Just a Cowboy's Princess

Flyboys of Sweet Briar Ranch in North Dakota
Book Eight
Jessie Gussman

Published By: Jessie Gussman

Contents

Acknowledgments

Cover art by Julia Gussman
Editing by Heather Hayden
Narration by Jay Dyess
Author Services by CE Author Assistant

Listen to a FREE professionally performed and produced audio-book version of this title on Youtube. Search for "Say With Jay" to browse all available FREE Dyess/Gussman audiobooks.

Chapter 1

The paparazzi had arrived.

Princess Kennedy Weaver-Payne, known as Kenni to her family and friends, froze on the sidewalk as three cars pulled up to the diner in Sweet Water, catty-corner across the street from where she was. People pouring out of all four doors, cameras around their necks, phones in hand, press badges lying like bull's-eyes on lanyards against their chests.

Thankfully they didn't glance her way. Possibly it was because of the short brown hair, or maybe the cheap five-dollar department store sunglasses, or maybe it was the prairie skirt and peasant blouse she wore.

Hardly the long blonde locks they were used to seeing, perfectly coiffured, the designer suits, and expensive matching pumps.

An outfit like she normally wore would draw their eye immediately but would definitely make her look out of place in this small town.

Regardless, the second-to-last person paused on the sidewalk, looking up at the sky before slowly turning.

Kenni's eyes opened wide, and her heart beat hard.

While she felt like her new look was different enough from her old one that she probably wouldn't be recognized, her brother would kill her if he knew she just stood on the sidewalk while the paparazzi poured out around her.

Seeing the big shaggy cow that her brother had told her was Sweet Water's own matchmaking steer, which had caused Kenni to roll her eyes at the antics small towns would go to in order to pull in tourism dollars, just up the street from where she stood, she took five big strides and ducked down behind it.

It had been standing in the same spot since she arrived with her brother in his pickup, contentedly chewing its cud, with its eyes half closed, looking like it had nothing better in the world to do than stand along the sidewalk in Sweet Water and soak up the summer sun.

Kenni had been a little jealous.

Billy, that's what Zeke, her brother, had said the steer's name was, was the town celebrity, and yet he could stand on the sidewalk in peace, no one criticizing his every move, critiquing his outfit, his mannerism, whether he smiled or didn't smile, and whether it was the right time to smile, or, worse than that, determining that it was somehow Billy's fault that his spouse had cheated on him.

The way Kenni's had cheated on her.

Pain went through her, not so much because she had been madly in love with her husband. But because she had trusted him, and his betrayal cut deep.

Taking a deep breath that shook as it entered her body, she tried to focus on the moment at hand, bending over and making sure that her entire body was hidden behind the steer, who hadn't seemed to notice that anything had changed in his life, or maybe he was just used to people crouching down behind him trying to hide themselves from the paparazzi that normally descended upon the small town.

Hardly.

Maybe she shouldn't have come. It seemed like such a quaint town. So old fashioned almost, and friendly. She hated to ruin those vibes with the sharks that circled the water around her, sensing blood and wanting to get a part of the kill.

"Excuse me. I'm going to assume that you're Kenni," a deep voice said above her.

If she hadn't been bent over, trying to hide herself behind the steer's body, obviously not acting like a normal person, she might have described the voice as...sexy.

Definitely the kind of voice that sent all the good shivers down her backbone and made her fingertips tingle.

One that actually sounded familiar.

Probably because she'd heard it shouting at her at some point to turn around so he could get a better picture.

The paparazzi had found her.

She reminded herself just in time not to move, even as her brain was saying that the paparazzi did not call her Kenni.

She was Princess Kennedy, and her name had never been shortened from the time Isaac had first introduced her to his world, until she had stepped out of it just a couple of months ago.

She tilted her head, maybe against her better judgment, to get a better look at the man who had come over and had just...crouched down beside her.

He had crouched.

He wore a T-shirt, which stretched over his shoulders, his brown neck showing that he spent time in the sun and similar brown arms that were roped with muscle.

Worn blue jeans.

Not exactly clothes the paparazzi usually wore when they chased her.

Plus, he had a cowboy hat pulled low over his eyes, like he used it to shade his face and not to make himself look good.

There was something familiar about the angle of his jaw.

"It's a risky thing to make assumptions," she finally said, not forgetting, even in her nervousness and insecurity, to use anything other than her most cultured voice.

"You don't sound like the Kenni I knew," the man said with a little bit of a grin.

"Who are you?" she asked, and though she might be crouching behind a cow, she wasn't going to beat around the bush.

Not that there were any bushes in sight.

"It was a long time ago. Your brother's in there dealing with the bottom-feeders, and he sent me out here to rescue you. But he forgot to hand me his keys, and my truck is parked behind the diner. So, we're going to have to figure out how to get you from here to there and make it look like you're supposed to be with me."

"You don't think they're gonna leave?" she asked, wanting to peek around the steer but knowing she shouldn't.

"They have your brother. They think you're with him. And they're not far off from the truth. Except, if I can get you out of here, you won't be."

"What makes you think I should go with you?"

"I'm a buddy of your brother's from the Air Force."

That was all he needed to say. She knew how much Zeke thought of his Air Force cronies. She also knew the code the men shared would keep them from doing anything to harm her.

Plus, while Zeke probably had a few guys who didn't like him, everyone did, they wouldn't be hanging out in Sweet Water. This man had come to keep her safe, and if there was any danger in the town itself, he would have said something.

The man's eyes were shadowed, but there was a hint of a smile around his lips as he looked at her, probably knowing that was all he had to say in order to make her trust him.

The man pulled a necklace out from around his neck, unhooking it and allowing something to drop in his hand.

"Do me a favor, take this ring and put it on your ring finger, and I'm gonna put my arm around you, and we're going to laugh together, like we're a couple. Princess Kennedy Weaver-Payne is not laughing with and married to someone else. Hopefully, anyone who glances in our direction will dismiss us as uninteresting. That should get us across the street and behind the diner to my pickup."

"What's plan B?" she asked, even as she took the ring he gave her and slid it onto the ring finger of her left hand. It was a little loose, but it would work.

"We depend on your disguise. Which, I have to say, is not that good. I'd recognize your nose anywhere."

"My nose?"

"I always had a thing for noses."

"Baker Lawrence?"

She couldn't believe it. Her brother's best friend, their neighbor in the small Virginia town they grew up in, and her childhood crush.

He was only two years older than she was, but she thought he'd hung the moon and painted the sunrises too.

She would never have told her husband, but she occasionally still dreamed about him. Not that she wanted to, just that she'd been so stuck on him for so many years.

He had been her first kiss.

"I'm not sure what that says about me that I mention my nose issue and you instantly recognize me."

"Maybe if you weren't wearing that ridiculous cowboy hat, I would have recognized you just by looking at you."

"Hmm. I'm not sure I want to be married to someone who thinks my hat is ridiculous."

"I'm not the one who asked you to marry me."

"I don't think I asked. I just gave you a ring and told you to pretend for a little bit."

"I guess it doesn't really matter what I think about your hat, since you hate my nose so much."

"I never said I hated your nose. Just that I recognized it." He glanced around the body of the steer, giving a jerk of his chin that she assumed meant the coast was clear.

He straightened, standing so the upper half of his body was visible to the paparazzi over the back of the steer who still stood in front of them.

She slowly followed him up. A lot more cautious, just because she knew how unshakable the paparazzi could be.

Of course, they had played in her favor at times as well. And they had come down squarely on her side when Isaac had cheated. Of course, Isaac was still the heir to the throne, and he would eventually be exonerated while she would fade into oblivion.

She had to admit she wouldn't mind it. The last ten years of constantly being in the eye of the world, her every move scrutinized, never knowing who she could trust, who would sell their soul, and her secrets, for whatever price the paparazzi was willing to pay, had taken a huge toll on her.

The worst, the very worst, was that she hadn't known who she could trust.

In this small town, she wanted to think that problem was over, but she wasn't entirely sure.

Regardless, she knew she could trust Baker. It was a good feeling.

Trying to do everything on her own had been exhausting.

"What in the world made you think I hated your nose?" Baker said as he looked down on her, waiting for her to straighten her clothes and brush her skirt off, just in case she picked up any dirt from the sidewalk.

"You always make fun of it."

"I never made fun of it. I always said it made you look aristocratic. Which was basically almost like fortune-telling since you ended up marrying an aristocrat."

"The biggest mistake of my life," she couldn't help but mutter.

"Sorry," Baker said, the teasing note out of his voice and true contrition entering it.

She appreciated that he felt bad for bringing it up, but she didn't want anyone to have to walk on eggshells around her. She wanted to be able to 'fess up to the mistakes she had made and not allow them to get her down.

Of course, the dissolution of the marriage she expected to last for a lifetime might take more than a few months to get over.

The pain was still fresh. The betrayal still cut deep. Her ability to trust might never recover.

After all, Isaac had been known as a very straightlaced and somewhat boring man who followed the rules. Did what he was told. Never stepped a foot out of line.

What had been so terrible about her that had made him feel like he couldn't stay in his marriage for whatever it was he needed from a woman?

That had been the question on everyone's mind, and she had read it more than once in the papers. And online.

Questioning whether she had been an absolute hag behind closed doors. Hag, nag, witch—she had all the names thrown at her. And it had finally gotten to her, how everyone thought it was her fault.

"All right, give me your hand, and then see if you can't put those latent acting skills to use."

"Latent acting skills?" she asked, scrunching her brows down, as she put her hand into his.

Despite the heat of the day, her fingers were cool, and she welcomed the warmth of his rough skin. The tingles that his voice had elicited multiplied as her fingers lay in his.

Thankful for her dark shades, she closed her eyes and looked away, ostensibly toward the diner where the vehicles that had spit out the paparazzi were still parked, squatting there as though claiming the ground for their own.

"Ready?"

"I don't understand what you said about my acting skills, but of course. I'm ready."

"You're going to have to act like you like me. Or at least, like you think I'm funny."

"I do like you. And I do think you're funny. Although it's been a long time, and I suppose you changed since I last spoke with you."

"That's news to me. I didn't think you liked me at all, and I really didn't think you thought I was funny. All of these compliments at one time are going to give a guy a big head."

"That's good. Maybe your hat will start fitting."

He barked out a laugh, and she smiled.

"If you don't like it, I can lose it," he said, taking his hat off and slapping his leg with it.

His hair was a little shorter than he'd worn it in high school, but his nose was exactly the same. A strong Roman nose that she'd teased him about just as much as he'd teased her about her aristocratic nose.

It was a little crooked, and he always claimed it was because his parents dropped him on his head when he was a baby.

She figured he probably fell down and hit it somewhere, but she'd never heard the story, if there even was one.

"I see your nose is still crooked," she murmured as they stepped around the steer.

"The one imperfect thing on my face, and she always zeroes in on it," he said, rather fatalistically.

"All right. Neutral territory. My brother said that steer is a matchmaking steer. I have to disagree, and I would say that he is more like a really good hiding spot."

"Actually, I'd need two hands to tell you all the couples in town that steer had a part in bringing together."

"Oh, so now you're on the tourism board in Sweet Water?" she asked with a raised brow.

He laughed and shook his head. "I know. We both come from small towns, and we know how they grasp at everything trying to get people to see their virtues. But I'm not kidding about this."

"Well, I have to say I'm unimpressed, not to mention, if he's going to be trying to matchmake me, he's going to be sadly disappointed."

"I don't know about that. We spent about two minutes together behind him, and now we're married." He lifted up the hand he held, the one with the ring on it, and she laughed. "Admit it. I'm right."

"It's a fake marriage. Just until we get across the street. After that, I'm gone."

She didn't mean that. She didn't take marriage vows so lightly. She couldn't even believe she was joking about it now. Especially after Isaac had played so fast and loose with his.

The sad thing was, she probably would have taken him back. Except he didn't want her. He wanted to be with the other woman.

She pushed those thoughts out of her head. She couldn't heal if all she did was pick her wounds open every time the thoughts came into her mind.

"Oh no," Baker said, causing her to pause and look up at him. He sounded truly horrified.

"What?"

"It's Miss April. And...it looks like she has her arm around one of the paparazzi."

Chapter 2

Baker couldn't believe he was standing in the street holding Kenni Weaver's hand. No, not Kenni. Not anymore. *Princess* Kennedy Weaver-Payne.

He'd jumped at the chance to get her away from the paparazzi. It hadn't been hard, with her disguise and his idea to be a couple. But he'd gotten lax. He should have been more careful, because there was no getting away from Miss April without causing a huge scene.

It wasn't Miss April he was worried about, but the woman beside her. From the lanyard around the woman's neck to the camera she held in her hand, it was a given she was one of the paparazzi.

Instead of rescuing Kenni like Zeke had asked and depended on him to do, he had led her right into the lion's den.

Miss April was just a couple yards away, and Baker didn't know what else to do. "I'm going to kiss you," he said, stopping and tugging on Kenni's hand.

It wasn't like it was a hardship. His first kiss had been behind the maple tree that stood on the boundary line between their yards. He'd been seventeen, she'd been fifteen, and he'd thought it was going to be the start of an amazing romance.

He wasn't sure what happened, but she had ended up running home crying. He didn't think she'd ever talked to him again.

It had been a huge blow to his ego. For a long time, possibly even now, he thought the problem was his kissing skills.

He'd figured for a while there was some kind of mysterious way that normal people kissed that he had never learned, and he had spent a lot of time listening to conversations, watching movies, reading any article he could get his hands on, trying to pick up clues on what he had done wrong.

He finally figured out that kissing wasn't something there was a manual for, but it really hadn't helped his confidence.

All of that went through his head as Kenni turned toward him, lifting her head.

She didn't protest, and maybe she understood, possibly from his panicked words, how serious this was.

If she wanted to hide in Sweet Water away from the eyes of the paparazzi, she was going to have to play along and be very, *very* convincing.

Honestly though, as his mouth descended on hers, and her hands wrapped around his shoulders, and he pulled her closer, he forgot all about trying to fool Miss April.

She felt a lot different than the beanpole she'd been when she was fifteen.

He supposed he probably did too.

But that really wasn't what he was thinking about as his hand wrapped around her waist, pulling her closer.

Somehow he must have dropped his hat because his other hand ended up buried in her short hair.

He'd liked the longer length but hadn't liked the fake blonde.

She'd been a dark brunette when he'd known her, and he liked her natural nut brown color much better than the platinum blonde locks that had been plastered on every grocery store magazine for the last ten years.

It seemed like everywhere he looked, he saw her face.

Her nose.

Her lips were soft under his, and maybe it was just his imagination, because he wanted it so much, but she seemed to press into him, pulling his head closer and making a little sound that gave him the idea that she was really enjoying their impromptu kiss and it wasn't just an act.

For him, his heart hammered in his chest, and his lungs wouldn't cooperate, seeming to be out of sync with the rest of his body, while his stomach twisted and turned, scared to death that he was going to make the same mistake he had all those years ago, when she'd run crying from him and left him standing there baffled, wondering what he'd done. But it only took a few more seconds before all of that faded away, and the woman in his arms was the only thing he thought about, how good she felt, her scent and her taste and the little sounds that she made. The way her breath was just as disjointed as his.

"Baker Lawrence, what in the world are you doing in the middle of the street? Don't you know this is a small town? There are children walking around."

It was Miss April's voice, but it took a little while to penetrate.

Baker lifted his head, his mouth hanging open, his eyes glazed. The only thing he could focus on was the face of the woman standing in front of him.

She looked just as confused as he felt, like her world had been shaken too, and she wasn't quite sure how she was to respond.

That's how he felt.

"That's the kiss I should have given you when you were fifteen."

His eyes stared into hers, and he waited for reality to snap back into place.

"Good thing you didn't," she said, and he wasn't sure what that meant. He didn't have time to question her further, because Miss April arrived beside them, huffing, with the lanyard woman beside her.

He swallowed, his throat dry, his heart still thundering in his chest.

He'd never had a kiss like that in his life before.

He wasn't done. Wasn't nearly done, certainly didn't want to stop to talk to Miss April.

But even though he'd grown up with Kenni, he barely knew the woman she'd become. Just knew what he'd seen of her on magazine shelves and what Zeke had told him. She wasn't his high school crush anymore. Far from it.

Miss April's words finally penetrated his brain, and he realized that the streets of Sweet Water were not the place to reacquaint himself with his high school crush.

"Baker? Are you deaf?" Miss April said.

"I was kissing my wife. Surely there aren't laws against that in town?"

He tried to have humor in his voice. Tried to have one side of his mouth tilt and lift an eyebrow at her, but his face felt frozen, his heart shaky, his feelings in turmoil.

"Your wife? When did you get married?" Miss April asked, her nose wrinkling like she couldn't believe that she had missed something so important.

"Last week."

"A year ago."

He pressed his lips together, containing his laugh, and looked at Kenni, who had taken it upon herself to answer that question with a different answer than the one he gave.

"It feels like a week," Baker clarified their lie.

Lying about anything didn't sit well. But this was for Kenni. To give her safety. She had been the object of an attempted abduction, and Zeke had insisted she come to Sweet Water, where he and his buddies from the Air Force could keep an eye on her.

He felt like all of his training had been in vain, and he was seventeen again, with no clue on how to do anything, whether it was kissing or keeping a person safe, but knowing that he found the one he wanted.

He had to push those feelings aside and try to protect her to the best of his ability.

"I didn't know you were married. That's interesting. Typically, all the unmarried men are on my radar. But you've been here for…how long?" Miss April tilted her head at him. "And I didn't even know." Her brows furrowed, and she turned her gaze toward Kenni. "Where have you been all this time?"

Kenni opened her mouth, but no sound came out.

Baker didn't wait more than a second before he spoke. "She's been on location."

"Oh? I don't recognize her as any type of movie star?" Miss April looked her up and down again. "Take off your glasses."

"She's not a movie star. She compares noses. I mean, she powders noses. Like, you know, makeup."

"Oh. A makeup artist. Interesting. While I would love to chat with you about that sometime—" Miss April paused, lifting her brows and looking at Baker as though expecting an introduction.

Right. Now he had to make up a name. He'd made such a terrible mess of making up a job for her. Noses.

Obviously, he wasn't used to lying.

"I am Emmaline Kendra." Kennedy rescued him.

He recalled that Emmaline was her middle name, and he was pretty sure Kendra was their mom's name. Smart. So he could still call her Kenni, and maybe people wouldn't figure anything out.

"Well, Emmaline, it's good to meet you. I'm glad you're back. I'm sure Baker has been very lonely without you."

"Yeah. So lonely that every once in a while, I just have to kiss her in the middle of the street, because I can't believe she's really back," Baker said, feeling stupid but also feeling like it was a really great excuse to have been caught kissing her.

"Well, maybe you guys better head home for a little bit then," Miss April said, winking, before she gasped. "Oh. I totally forgot to introduce you to my niece. This is Eliza. She has a job with a newspaper in Austin, Texas, but she's been thinking about relocating to Sweet Water. I told her how friendly the town was and how much I'd like to have her around, and I think I'm wearing her down."

"I just have to sell one big picture, and I'll be able to make the move," Eliza said, looking a lot more friendly than Baker had thought anyone who was a part of the paparazzi would look.

She actually looked sweet and cute. A little on the young side, maybe, but definitely the kind of girl who could get used to small-town life.

"Welcome to Sweet Water," he said. "I've found it to be a great place. And I can't wait to set up house with my wife." He put his arm around Kenni, pulling her close against his side.

"I'm sure the town isn't going to be able to wait to be introduced to her and to hear all about the adventures she's had on different movie sets. I'm sure she has a lot of stories we'd all love to hear."

"I'm sure she does," Baker said, unwilling to leave Kenni to the wolves trying to figure out something to say to that lie.

He was going to have to keep Kenni out of town for a while, not just to keep her from being recognized but to keep her from being asked about her "job." It was all his fault.

He owed her an apology. Not just for lying about her job, but for the kiss as well. However, hopefully she agreed with him that the whole thing was necessary. After all, they had discovered after her almost-abduction that the person who had paid to have her kidnapped had been willing to have her killed if the ransom demands had not been met.

It had been a scary time, for Zeke especially, and was what had prompted him to bring her to Sweet Water.

No one thought the paparazzi would follow her halfway around the world to Sweet Water.

How had they known?

Something Kenni had dealt with that he wasn't used to was people who were not loyal. People who would sell information about the people they were supposed to love, just to make money.

So sad.

"I heard so many good things about this town. Baker just raves about what a wonderful place Sweet Water is. I can't wait to get to know everyone."

Miss April nodded her head knowingly. "I'm sure that Baker has told you about our matchmaking steer. If you have any unmarried friends, be sure to bring them, because Billy can match anyone."

"You know, when Baker first told me about Billy, I thought it was a joke. But now that I've been in Sweet Water, I actually think it might be true."

She tilted her head up and looked at Baker who had to fight back a laugh. After all, Billy hadn't even broken a sweat matching Kenni up with Baker. She'd stood beside him, and five minutes later, she was kissing and "married" to him.

"I told you I wasn't exaggerating about Billy's skills," Baker couldn't help but say.

"Although I didn't see the pig that is supposedly the love interest of poor Billy."

"She has babies at a house just outside of town. If Baker is giving you the grand tour, make sure he takes you there. They're used to people coming and seeing them."

"I'll have to make sure he shows me." Kenni smiled without showing her teeth. She looked directly at Eliza, holding her hand out. "It's nice to meet you, Eliza. Welcome to Sweet Water, although I recommend staying away from Billy if you're not interested in getting married. He acts fast."

Eliza looked a little confused, but she put her hand out and shook Kenni's. "I'll keep that in mind. Although, I guess I can understand your reluctance to believe a story about a matchmaking steer, since I have the same reticence."

"This is one of those cases where common sense will not be correct," Kenni said. "Now, if you two don't mind, I had a long trip and I'm tired. Baker promised to take me out to the ranch and allow me to rest and recover. We had some very long days on set." She eyed Baker. "And I'm definitely looking forward to a little peace and quiet and some time to relax."

"You might not want to do it on the ranch." Miss April looked concerned. "From what I've heard, Sweet Briar has been a hive of activity as they're putting together a bunch of things to try to create a dude ranch out there. Not that anyone around Sweet Water minds. We're all about whatever is going to bring in the tourism dollars and help the rest of us keep our jobs."

"It has been busy," Baker admitted. "But I'm going to make sure that Kenni gets some rest." Now that he knew she'd be on the ranch.

"Kenni?" Miss April said, her eyes more shrewd than Baker had given her credit for. "I thought you said her name was Emmaline?"

"It is. But did you hear my middle name is Kendra? My close friends and family call me Kenni."

"I see. Well, that explains it," Miss April said, the suspicion not totally out of her expression, but her smile genuine.

Baker slid his hand into Kenni's, and they waved as they walked away from Miss April and Eliza.

"I can't believe they didn't recognize you," Baker said, after they'd walked between the diner and the building next to it to the lot in the back where his truck was parked.

"I can't believe it either, but I'm glad I had the cheap glasses and that I cut and dyed my hair."

"I think the small-town clothes probably helped as much as anything. People aren't expecting Princess Kennedy Weaver-Payne to wear anything less than the best."

"Actually, I really like these clothes. This is about the most comfortable thing I've worn in years," Kenni said, and he smiled at her tone. It held wonder but also humor, and it was what he remembered she'd sounded like, not the snotty tone she'd used earlier.

"You look good in it," he said, walking her over to the passenger side of his truck to open the door for her. Her body jerked at his compliment.

It surprised him that she seemed to be shocked that he might give her a compliment. Maybe that meant she didn't realize he wasn't acting during their kiss. It had rocked him from the bottom of his toes to the backside of his heart. No one could be that good of an actor.

But maybe Kenni was. Maybe she really was acting.

"It was nice to see that you didn't run away crying that time," he said as he opened the door and held it while she climbed in his truck.

"Possibly that's because you didn't whisper some other woman's name in the middle of our kiss," she said, raising her eyebrows haughtily and giving him a look that made him feel about two inches tall, before she grabbed the door handle and slammed it shut. He stepped quickly back out of the way.

Well, rats. Is that what he had done? He hadn't realized.

But that answered his question as to whether she'd been acting during their kiss. It had obviously been an artifice on her part, because she certainly wasn't happy with him now.

Chapter 3

Kenni sat in the truck while Baker walked around.

She had a policy in her life to never lie. And here she was in Sweet Water, barely been in town for half an hour, and she'd lied more in the last thirty minutes than she'd lied in the last ten years.

She hated it.

But she also understood why Baker had said what he had and done what he did.

Her lips still tingled from the kiss, and she finally did what she had wanted to do ever since he'd raised his head, and that was to touch her fingers to her lips, almost as though to make sure they were still there. Or that they hadn't caught fire or something. She wasn't sure exactly what, but... It'd been ten years since she kissed any man other than Prince Isaac, her husband. And the only man she kissed before that was Baker. If she could call seventeen-year-old Baker a man.

He'd certainly been mature for his age.

She wasn't sure whether she was any judge of kissing skills with her limited experience, but if she had to compare Baker and Isaac, Baker won hands down, even seventeen-year-old Baker.

Not that the way a man kissed said anything about his character. Now that she was older and hopefully a little wiser, she certainly cared more about a man's character than his kissing ability.

Still, Baker had a way of turning her world upside down.

And that had been a fake kiss. Something he'd done to protect her, to guard her, because he took his job seriously. When he had told her brother that he would take care of her, he had meant that he would do whatever was necessary to make sure she got out of town unrecognized.

Even if that meant kissing her.

"I know your brother's going to hear about that," Baker said as he climbed in the other side of the pickup.

She yanked her fingers away from her lips and looked out the windshield of the truck, not wanting to give in to the temptation to let her eyes just sit on him, watching as he moved.

His movements were short, strong, confident.

Isaac had been confident as well, but his movements had been more choreographed. Baker was wilder somehow. She couldn't exactly explain it, but the difference in them, although they were both strong, confident men, was night and day.

After being married to Isaac, she would choose Baker any day.

Again, it wasn't necessarily because of his wildness, or his manliness, or the way he looked, or even the way he kissed, even if he did make her knees weak and her heart flutter with just the thought of it.

It was his character that she appreciated. The fact that he was loyal to his friend, no matter what.

Of course, there was the lie.

"It's a small town," she said easily. She'd grown up in one, maybe not as small as Sweet Water, but she knew how they were.

"Exactly. And they're going to hear that we said we were married. Or that I said I was married, and they're going to figure out that the person I'm supposed to be married to is you."

"They'll understand why."

"I know. I just... I hate that there is a lie sitting there. One I can't correct. I have to allow it to stand. And I don't resent that." He looked across the console after he had started his truck, giving her a glance that said he was sincere. "I'd say it all again. Just to protect you. But I hate lying."

"Me too. But after you said it, I knew it was the best way. And for me to say anything that contradicted what you said would just bring more attention to me. So, if you're feeling guilty for my sake, don't."

"I know Zeke is going to understand, but he's not going to like it."

"That whole best friend's little sister deal?"

"Not really," Baker said as he turned the truck around and then pulled out on the street. "It's more that I was supposed to protect you, not marry you. You're not really supposed to get involved with the people who are under your care. It's...kind of like taking advantage of them."

"I wasn't under your care. I was doing just fine on my own, thank you."

"Yeah. Scrunched down behind Billy. That was...really taking matters in your own hands there and being proactive."

"It was working."

"My way worked, too."

"Yeah, but now we're entangled in something we don't know how to get out of."

"Surely this all is going to die down." His words seemed to be a statement, but they actually sounded like a question.

She responded to the tone more than the words. "I don't know. I...I seem to be a favorite of the tabloids. Anything that they can get on me helps sell stories and makes them money. I hardly think they're going to give a lucrative career up, especially since the harder I am to photograph, the more valuable photographs of me will be."

She didn't want to sound like a Debbie Downer, but it was true. It was almost like America had gotten addicted to hearing about "their" princess.

Corinth was a small country. Most people had never heard of it until ten years ago when Sir Isaac Payne had snagged himself an American commoner to marry. It was the first time in the country's history that royalty had stepped out of the country to find themselves a bride.

There were no laws against it, and Isaac's parents, Queen Isabella and King Henry, had been all for it. Anything that got their country attention and brought tourists in, along with their pocketbooks, was welcome.

Queen Isabella had told her more than once that her marriage had saved their kingdom.

It had brought renewed interest and attention to their small country and had enabled them to revive their flagging tourism business.

"Zeke isn't going to want to let you run around by yourself," Baker said, muttering more to himself than actually having a conversation, almost as though he were thinking about it.

"No. After the abduction attempt, particularly when they found out that the man who tried to take me had told his accomplices that if the ransom wasn't paid, he was killing me, Zeke was scared."

"Of course he was." The town of Sweet Water had faded in the distance, and he slowed to make a left. "It scared all of us."

"You haven't seen me for years."

"I've seen your picture. You look a little different in the tabloids than you do right now, but still."

She rolled her eyes, then looked out the window. Of course she looked different. She never stepped out of the palace without her hair and makeup being perfect. Her clothes had been carefully chosen and every outing had been scripted.

She hadn't really minded the stifling atmosphere in the palace. It had been pleasant and had been a lot different than what she was used to, but she understood the necessity of it. She had understood what she was getting into when she married Isaac. That there was always going to be the fact that he was going to be king between them and there were protocols that had to be followed.

It hadn't been rocket science. Although, the extent to which her life had been changed and controlled had surprised her.

Still, she had agreed to it when she married him, and she intended to keep her word.

Unfortunately, he hadn't kept his.

"So…" Baker drew the word out. "Do you have any ideas of how you want to handle this?"

"I think I'll leave that up to you. The idea to say we were married was yours. And I'm pretty sure the kiss was your idea as well."

She snapped her mouth closed before she said something more about the kiss. Something she didn't want him to know. Like how much she enjoyed it.

"Ouch. All right. That's the truth. I'll own it."

"I'll support you," she said, feeling bad that she'd thrown everything in his lap when all he'd been doing was trying to protect her. "You know I will."

He didn't know any such thing. He hadn't talked to her for a decade. Of course, he knew her brother and knew her growing up. She hadn't changed that much. Her character hadn't changed, anyway.

"I don't know that I did. You're much different than you were when you were a kid."

"How so?" she asked, her head turning toward him.

"Well. You used to be this tall tomboy who was forever chasing us around. You played football with us, went fishing, jumped off the railroad bridge outside of town. But now… You wear designer clothes and stand in front of microphones and cameras and pet kids on the head or whatever you do."

"Pet kids on the head?" she asked, shaking her head and laughing despite herself. "I have a children's charity I support. I support a lot of charities. I bring attention to them with my presence, and it helps people remember that they need to donate to good causes."

"Like I said, you go around patting kids on the head. You didn't used to do that."

"All right. I'll give you that. I didn't used to do that."

"And you didn't used to admit that you were wrong. That's new, too."

"You can say it. I was stubborn. I... I might still be a little bit stubborn, but not like I used to be."

After all, when her husband said he wanted to choose Susan over her, she didn't fight him. She didn't even demand any kind of divorce settlement beyond what he offered. Even though her advisors said he'd lowballed her thinking she'd make a counteroffer. She allowed it to go through. One of the fastest divorces she'd ever witnessed. She stepped aside to make things as easy for Isaac as possible, and for the king and queen as well, whom she'd grown to love.

They didn't have a choice. They had to support their son. And so, while she hadn't exactly been thrown out in the cold, it had been close.

After years of being forced to depend on them to take care of her, she felt bereft when they were no longer concerned over what was best for her nor made decisions with her best interests at heart, behind the interest of the future of the monarchy.

At least there hadn't been children.

She had begged Isaac to go to a fertility doctor to see if there was something they could do. But he hadn't been interested.

"I guess I'll have to see that change to believe it," Baker murmured.

"Really? I'm supposed to just believe everything you say, but you have to see proof to believe me?"

"What did I ask you to take on trust?"

"Everything we've done. You took my hand and started dragging me across the street, telling me I had to agree to be your wife, then you kissed me and started telling the townspeople I was a makeup artist. It took a certain amount of trust to go along with that."

"You're right. I'm sorry. I'll believe you. You're not stubborn."

"Whoa. Wait. I did not say I wasn't stubborn. I just said I wasn't as stubborn as I used to be."

"All right. Not as stubborn. That's kind of subjective though."

"Exactly. So no matter how you look at it, I'm right."

"I take it back about being able to admit that you're wrong."

"Yeah. That doesn't come easy either. I want the rest of the world to be wrong, as long as I'm still right."

"I think that's the same with everybody."

They drove in silence for a little bit, her looking at the flat North Dakota landscape, stretching out as far as she could see. It was pretty this time of year. Green. Lush. Although Zeke had told her that it got brown fast when it got hot and dry in the summer.

"I suppose he told you about the farm?"

"A little. He said I would see it when I got there. You know how Zeke is. Sometimes he doesn't talk much."

"He was probably concentrating on getting you here without losing you."

"Yeah. The abduction really upset him."

"He's probably not going to want to leave your side once we get you to the farm. Or he might try to lock you in the house. Zeke can be a little bit obsessive. So, if you want a tour, I can give you one when we get there."

"You're probably right," she said, not even laughing, because it was true. Zeke wasn't going to want her to show her face anywhere without an armed escort. Which she would say was overkill, but maybe it wasn't. As much as she laughed off the abduction, she really had no desire to die. She wanted to reinvent her life. Wanted to show that she didn't need Prince Isaac, nor his kingdom, in order for her to be successful and happy.

She wasn't exactly sure what successful and happy looked like, but it definitely looked like something that didn't include Isaac and his girlfriend anyway.

"Does that mean you want a tour?"

"I don't want you to have to spend more time babysitting me. I'm sure you have things to do."

"Actually I do. And you can come along and give me a hand."

He said it a little sarcastically, like he wasn't actually expecting her to do anything that was going to help him.

"I might have been a princess, but that doesn't mean I can't work." Surely he knew that. He'd seen her growing up. He knew that her parents were working-class, regular folk, with her dad working in construction and her mom working as an administrative assistant to a small business in town.

"I thought maybe you'd forgotten how. You've lived a lavish lifestyle. All those heads you had to pat."

"Would you stop?" She half laughed, but she crossed her arms over her chest too. "You're going to totally blow my cover if you continue to act like I used to be a princess."

"But you were."

"I'm not anymore. I'm just a regular American, who is, apparently, living on a farm now. So, if there's work to be done, I can do it. After all, the sooner I get my hands all callused and get my clothes mucked up, the less I'll look like a princess, and the harder I'll be to spot and the less I'll stand out."

His shoulders slumped a bit. "That's a good point. And I'm sorry. You just...look like a princess."

She fingered her short hair. That was probably the one thing she missed the most. But she figured it hadn't been enough to dye it brown, she had to have a new do, something completely opposite from what she had. So, her hair was so short the beautician had shaved her neck.

"I miss my long hair," she said, hating the emotion that came out of her voice. It was just hair.

"It will grow back," he said, and the words could have been said almost dismissively, but they weren't. He looked over, and the expression on his face said that he had heard the emotion in her voice and cared.

Of course, the king and queen had cared too. As long as she was under their care and in their charge. But their loyalty had stopped with Isaac, and honestly, their betrayal probably hurt just as much as his.

Not that they betrayed her, exactly, but if there were sides, they'd most definitely sided with their son. As they needed to, but Kenni hadn't been the one who had been wrong.

"I know." She supposed they were talking about her hair, but she knew that time would heal the wounds. Time would help her be able to trust again. Time would make it not hurt so bad. The betrayal, the way they had circled the wagons around their son and left her out in the cold. The way she felt like she was a commodity that could be dumped when they no longer had a need for her.

Although she understood exactly why the royal family had done what they did and knew that it was necessary in order for them to preserve the institution, it still hurt.

"I guess I need to read up a little more on what exactly happened. You...look sad."

"Maybe I'm just sad because you don't think I've got what it takes to be a farm girl."

Chapter 4

"I never said that," Baker said, looking truly surprised.

"That's what you were insinuating."

"No. I'm sorry. I was just teasing you. You're a princess, and I'm a little intimidated, to be honest. Even though we grew up together, you...you had a completely different life than I have, and while I love the farm and actually feel very much at home here, I thought that it might be a little bit beneath you."

"No!" she said immediately.

In Corinth, she'd been known as the People's Princess. Because she hadn't been afraid to get her hands dirty, wherever she'd gone. When at an orphanage, she changed diapers, had babies spit on her, and spent time in the dirt playing with the toddlers and preschoolers, and when at an assisted living center, she visited with the residents and put puzzles together with them, swept their halls and served their food.

It was something that the people of Corinth hadn't been used to in their princess, and while she caught some flak for it, for the most part the king and queen had been happy to have someone who was so relatable to their subjects. Isaac had perhaps felt like she was more popular than he was and was possibly jealous.

She wasn't sure. She certainly hadn't done anything on purpose to try to make him look less in the eyes of the subjects.

Her goal in everything had always been to support him and to support the crown and the institution.

After all, she didn't want to marry into it, just to destroy it. That was foolish.

Every wise woman buildeth her house: but the foolish plucketh it down with her hands.

That verse popped into her mind. That's what she always tried to do. Build her husband's house. After all, when she built her husband up, she was building her own home as well.

That seemed to be an outdated idea, but she had thrown herself into it with everything she had.

Isaac hadn't seen it that way though.

And apparently, without her even realizing it, she was intimidating to Baker. Of all people.

"You seem like you're much too competent to be intimidated by someone like me."

"By a princess?"

"I'm not a princess anymore, remember?"

"But you were."

"A title really doesn't mean anything, does it?"

"It does."

She had to concede his point. "It's important. Maybe here in America, we don't understand it as much, but from the decade that I spent in Corinth, I learned it really does mean something. And once it's taken away, you truly are no longer a princess."

"Yeah, I guess you're right. That's hard for me to fathom. You are what you are, no matter what your title is."

"That's a very American way of thinking." She smiled. She felt it was the right way to think, but that wasn't necessarily the way the rest of the world lived.

"Here's where we turn to get to the farm. There's a big farmhouse, and that's where Darby and Jonah live with Amber, their daughter. We moved out to give them some privacy since they just got married. The house we live in isn't nearly as nice nor as large."

"By 'we,' you mean you and Zeke?"

"Yeah. And Miller. Gideon had been living there with us, but he just married Piper and moved into her house. I think eventually they'd like to move back to the farm, since their kids would really enjoy living there."

"Their kids?"

"They have six. Actually, Piper had six, but her husband died. It's a long story. You could probably fill a book with it, but just suffice it to say that Gideon acts like they're his. And he acts like Piper is the only woman in the world. So, if you talk to him, he probably won't see you."

"All right. I like that. I wish my husband had acted like that."

It wasn't exactly a joke. The words were serious, but she said them with a smile. Even if there was a small ache in her heart when she spoke them. After all, the wound was still fresh.

"Yeah. I heard about that. The guy's an idiot."

"Maybe." She supposed Baker was talking about the way Isaac had gotten caught with his girlfriend. It hadn't exactly been a regal way to announce to the world that he was cheating on his wife. If there was such a thing.

"What work do we have to do?" she asked, just because she didn't want to think about Isaac and Susan anymore.

Chapter 5

"The boys have a crop-dusting service. And that's pretty much what the rest of the guys are working on right now. We have two hundred cattle, and I've been the one doing most of the work with them, just because I was the only one who had any experience working with cattle before. We hope to hire help, but we decided that for this year we would try to get everything done ourselves. To save the money that we would normally pay hired guys and try to get most of our debts paid down. We're working on setting up a dude ranch, and since we were all in construction..." He smiled and shook his head. There he was, rambling on, and her eyes were probably crossing and he was boring her to tears. "That wasn't answering your question, was it?"

"You can keep going. I'm interested. If I'm going to be living here, even for a short while, I'd like to know what I can do to help. I definitely can't do anything with crop dusting. Whatever that is."

"It involves flying airplanes and mixing chemicals, and you're right. You probably can't help with that. Darby keeps the books at the office at the main farmhouse." They were driving up to it, flower beds blooming in profusion, since Darby had taken over. "The last two years, those flower beds had been nothing but weeds, but Darby coaxed them to life."

"They're beautiful. She has quite a touch."

"Jonah has been helping her. But yeah. She spends a lot of time with them, because she just loves it, I guess."

"It's nice when you find something that you love, and it's something that you're good at, and you have results like that." She smiled again at the flowers.

"Maybe you'll find something like that here," he said, hoping it was true. He wanted her to be happy. The clouds of sadness that seemed to take over her expression from time to time touched his heart and made him want to defend her. But he didn't know what he was defending her against. It wouldn't be the abduction—that might scare her, but it wouldn't make her sad. Plus, it was over.

Had she really loved her husband? He'd heard he'd cheated on her. Was she still reeling from a broken heart?

He took a breath, trying to focus his thoughts. Whether her heart was broken or not was none of his business. As much as he wanted it to be, apparently.

He needed to remember that this was Zeke's sister. The princess. Just because she was his childhood crush, just because being with her made him feel like he'd finally, truly come home, didn't mean that he was going to get to spend any time with her.

"Zeke might want to stay home, now that you're here. I can do his job. But I'm not sure how he'll do with mine."

"Because he doesn't know anything about cows?"

"Yeah. There's a bit of a learning curve. And you can kill them if you don't take care of them properly. That's what I was going to do when we get home. I have two bottle babies that need to be fed."

"Bottle babies?"

"One is a twin whose mother wouldn't take him. She took his sister."

"Ouch. That's harsh."

"Yeah. We'll get one or two of those each year. But you're good with orphans. You can pat heads."

"Stop it."

He smiled, glad she was laughing. It was the only thing he'd found so far that he could tease her about to make her chuckle.

"The other one just wouldn't suck when he was born. It took a little while until I got him so that he would eat, but by then, his mom didn't want him anymore."

"That's sad."

"It is. But it happens. I'm just happy they're both surviving. But while they're small, I like to see them get three or four small bottles a day, rather than two big ones. That's what they graduate to when they get a little older. Two meals makes it easier on me. But while I'm able to, I give them at least one middle-of-the-day feeding. That'll help them pick up a little better."

"That's probably what they get from their mom. More small meals, rather than two big ones?"

"That's right," he said, impressed that she'd figured that out.

"I was just guessing. From my experience patting children's heads."

"Hmm. I thought that would have been wasted experience. I'm impressed that you're able to translate that knowledge into something that can be used here on the farm."

"You never know when knowing how to pat heads can come in handy."

They laughed together, and he liked the way it made him feel. Like they were friends.

Even as he told himself to be careful. She was not someone who was going to fall for someone like him. She'd been married to royalty. Once she'd gotten herself situated, licked her wounds, and recovered, she'd be back out doing something to conquer the world.

"This is our house," he said as they pulled in and he shut the pickup off. "I told you Gideon just moved out, so there's one bedroom available. They're small, and the house isn't in great shape. We did a lot of work to it over the winter, but there's still more work to be done."

"That's fine. I don't need anything fancy. Hopefully I have a bed?"

"There's a bed. And clean sheets. The bathroom sink doesn't leak anymore, and I fixed the hole in the ceiling of your room too."

"That's good to know."

"We do still have a bit of a mouse problem. They seem to be wise to poison, so we have two cats."

"They catch mice?"

"Actually, no. We got them hoping that they would, but they're just more companions than mousers. I'm still hoping. Meanwhile, the mice are multiplying."

"All right. So we have cats and mice in the house?" she asked, her brows lifted.

"Yes. That was what I was getting at. Cats, mice, and that's my heeler, Boomer."

She looked over at the dog who was coming out from underneath the porch. "Boomer?"

"Yeah. The breeder gave him that name, and I kept it."

"So you got him on purpose?"

He laughed. "He's not much to look at, but he's got good herding instincts, and since I'm doing this mostly by myself, I figured I needed someone to give me a hand. I'm not much of a horse rider, although I'm getting better. But if a man has a good cow horse and a good herding dog, he can do a lot more than three men without a horse and dog."

"I see."

He didn't add that with a good wife, a man would be set for life. After all, that wasn't exactly a modern thing to say. Most women wouldn't want to be lumped in with a man's horse and his dog.

At least from Baker's experience.

But on the farm, a wife needed to be all in with her husband. Not sending him off while she did her own thing.

Probably that was why he wasn't even trying to find a wife. As much as he might like one. After all, what woman wanted to settle down on the farm and be a farmer's wife? There was no glory in that.

Just a lot of hard work.

"So Boomer herds cattle?" she asked, with her hand on the door latch. "And doesn't bite princesses?"

"Boomer's not going to bite you. He's hyper, which he needs to be in order to have the energy to do his work. But he's not mean. And to answer your question, he's got great herding instincts, and he's doing a great job, but training him takes time and I'm still working different aspects. I've never trained a dog before, so there's a lot of reading material in the house on dog training, if you're interested."

"Are you trying to pawn off the dog training on me?"

"Not really. But if you're interested..."

She laughed. And he smiled. He liked that she seemed to have loosened up and had become more accepting of him.

He hadn't meant to kiss her two seconds after he met her again for the first time in ten years. It just seemed the prudent thing to do at the time. But it seemed to have stifled their relationship a little too. Maybe he should explain to her that it hadn't meant anything.

That would be a lie, though. Because while he hadn't meant for it to mean anything, it didn't change the fact that it did.

Chapter 6

Kenni pulled the door latch and slid out of the truck.

Baker hadn't lied about the house being small, but she was charmed nonetheless. After living in a palace for ten years, she would never stop appreciating how nice it was to pull up to a house and get out with no fanfare. No cameras. No one wanting to make sure she smiled at all the right people and didn't trip.

The place just felt like home. Even with the wind whipping down across the prairie. Actually, she kind of liked the wind. It gave character to the land. She would guess that at different times of the year, the wind felt different.

She looked forward to finding out.

Of course, after she had laid low for a while, she needed to pull her life back together and figure out something to do.

She had left her American life for Isaac, put everything on the back burner to support her husband.

Now, she wasn't sure exactly what she was going to do.

She supposed she could use her fame to perpetuate good causes, but...did she want to continue in that lifestyle?

Also, she didn't want to overshadow Isaac, nor the king and queen, who, despite the fact that they had hurt her, she still loved.

They might see her stepping out into the limelight as trying to steal their thunder.

"Good boy," Baker said to Boomer as he yapped around his feet.

"Does he always bark that much?" Kenni asked. She walked around the pickup and stood a few feet away, watching Baker and his dog.

"Yeah. He's yappy. But that's okay since we're so far out. It's actually probably a good thing. Especially with you here."

"I hope I don't disrupt your routine too much," she said, thinking for the first time that having her there might be a problem.

Her brother had insisted on it, and she hadn't argued. The palace had funded guards for her until their divorce was final. Her attempted abduction had happened three months after that. She had requested to have a guard reinstated, but her request had been denied by the palace and the kingdom of Corinth.

"We'll see what he says. But I don't see a problem with anything. We'll probably just keep a closer eye on things, and like I said, he'll probably want you to stay home."

Maybe she should go somewhere else. Somewhere where she wouldn't be putting anyone out.

He and Zeke had said how they were trying to start a dude ranch, and things were busy. Surely she would just be holding people back?

Unless she found a place for herself and a job to do.

Baker stood from where he was petting his dog. "Are you ready to go see the calves?"

"I might as well. All of my bags were in my brother's truck. I have nothing else to do."

"Are you thirsty or hungry?"

"No. I'm good."

He looked at her for a second, as though judging whether or not that was true, and then he said, "Follow me."

She expected him to head toward the barn, but he didn't. He walked around the side of the house.

"We mix the bottles in here. The barn doesn't have hot water, and it gets cold enough in the winter that it's not really feasible anyway. Plus, it's a lot nicer to mix the bottles here than it is to do it out in the cold."

"A lot of what you do must be focused around how cold it gets."

"Yeah. The cold is a major player. Especially for a farmer."

"That's one of the things he mentioned. That it gets really cold here."

"We don't have to worry about that for a few months at least. We'll have a nice hot summer, a short fall, and then things will freeze again. But I kind of like that too. The cold makes the air feel clean and fresh."

She could tell by the way he looked that he loved living in North Dakota. She figured it probably took a certain kind of person to love the harsh weather, but it was certainly a pretty country.

He showed her how to scoop the milk replacer out of the garbage can where they kept it. "We have it sitting out here on the porch so it doesn't take up any room inside, but that means we have to keep the lid on tight, not only so it doesn't get wet, but so that no rodents get in it as well."

"I assume by rodents you are not talking about the cute kind but the ones with nasty teeth and tails."

"That is a correct assumption," Baker said, lifting his brow at her before he opened the door and allowed her to walk in first.

He let the water run until it was warm and filled the bottle up about half full before he shook it.

"You want to shake it well, because you don't want to have any chunks in the milk. They won't come out very well, and you want to make sure the calves get all the nutrition they're supposed to have."

"Got it. Shake the bottle a lot."

"And that's it. Once you have them mixed well, we'll head out."

It was a little tricky getting the nipples on top of the bottles because they had to be tight in order not to fall off, which made sense to Kenni, although it made them harder to put on.

"We keep the babies close to the house, in this pen right next to the barn. In the summer and the winter, the barn provides shelter, and in the summer, it provides shade."

"I see. Do you have calves year-round?"

"We didn't have any last winter, because we just bought our herd. But the man we bought them from said about one hundred fifty or so would calve this spring, and then he had fifty that would calve in the fall. That makes it nice. We'll have calves to sell at two different times of the year, instead of just once. It makes it a little easier to have less cows calving at one time."

"So how does he get them all to get pregnant at the same time?" she asked and felt a little embarrassed when Baker smiled. She had thought it was a legitimate question.

"We'll put the bull in for two months, maybe three. When we take him out, the cows that aren't bred will go into the fall herd, and they'll get bred then. If they go through four to six months with the bull, and they don't get bred, we'll sell them."

"You'll sell them? To whom?"

That time, he did laugh. "To whoever will buy them. But we can't make a living, we can't pay our bills, if we keep cows that don't have calves. So, if we end up with one that won't get pregnant, we need to get rid of her."

"I see." She wasn't sure that she entirely saw, but maybe that wasn't something that she was going to have to worry about. She certainly would love to take care of the babies, but deciding which mama cows stayed and which ones went wasn't something she really wanted to have to deal with.

"Oh my goodness, they're so cute!" she said when they walked around the side of the barn and saw the two cute little babies standing at the gate, bawling that they were hungry.

The babies were black with snow-white faces, and they couldn't have been more than two and a half or three feet tall.

They looked skinny too.

"You're only feeding them half a bottle?" she asked. "They look skinny to me."

"Yeah. As they get older, we'll give them more. But you don't want to feed them too much. That's an area where people often make a mistake. You naturally want to feed them as much as they'll eat, which is a lot more than half a bottle right now. But baby calves will get sick fast from eating too much, but they'll survive better than you think by eating much less than you think they need. So, while it's kind of a natural thing to want to feed them a lot, you really have to fight that. Or you'll lose them."

"I see. That's so weird. Human babies don't get sick by eating as much as they want."

"That's true, they don't. I wonder if it's healthy for them?"

"I don't know. Isn't that what parents do? They cry, so we feed them."

"You do pretty much anything to keep them from crying, right?"

"That's right," she said, watching as he held the bottle out to her.

"You want to feed them?"

She looked at the bottle, but it only took a split second before she decided that she definitely wanted to.

"Sure," she said, taking the bottle.

She watched as he held the other bottle upright until one calf sniffed it and then took it in its mouth.

She tried to do the same for hers, but her calf was looking at his and trying to get its mouth on his nipple, even though the other calf was already sucking on it. It didn't want to pay any attention to hers.

"Sometimes you have to put your hand in its mouth to try to get its attention to where you want it to go." Baker spoke as he stuck a finger in the calf's mouth. Right away, her calf started sucking his finger and forgot all about the bottle the other calf had.

"Now, stick your nipple where my finger is."

"Just shove it in his mouth?"

"Pretty much. Don't do it hard, but you can give it a good push."

A good push was a little bit more effort than what she did at first, but when her first efforts didn't manage to get the bottle in the calf's mouth, she pushed harder until it did.

As soon as her calf started to taste the milk when she tilted the bottle up, it sucked like its little life depended on it.

"They're so hungry."

"They act like they're starved pretty much all the time. But remember what I said. It's important that you don't overfeed them."

"It doesn't matter whenever they're on their mom? Or their moms don't give this much milk?"

"For beef cows, like these are, you usually don't have to worry about it. Their moms don't produce so much milk that there's any danger of them being overfed. And they get small meals throughout the day. But in all my experience, I've never seen a calf get sick from getting too much milk from its mom, no matter how much milk she has. I've seen them get sick when they've sucked on a cow that isn't their mom and gotten too much. And I've lost more than a few when they've gotten too much milk replacer."

"Lost them. They died?"

"Yeah. It'll kill them."

He had emphasized that almost the entire time they'd been out there. She had to believe it was true.

It seemed like less than a minute before the bottles were completely drained, and the calves were sucking empty air.

"Do we have to burp them or anything?" she asked, hoping that wasn't a dumb question.

He laughed, so she figured it probably was.

"Nope. And it won't hurt them at all to keep sucking at an empty bottle, unlike a baby, I guess."

"Yeah. And babies can't burp. They need their backs patted or something." She'd never actually had any of her own, of course, but Isaac's sister had had a baby while she had been at the castle.

Of course, she had a nurse for it and only had it around when she needed it for a photo op.

Kenni hadn't talked to the king and queen, but she had assumed that it would be her choice as to whether or not she wanted to spend more time with her baby.

She would have insisted on it, had the situation arisen, but since she and Isaac had been unable to conceive, the situation had never been up for discussion.

"I always take the bottles back and wash them out real good. I have a bottle brush sitting on the sink, but I don't use that every time. A lot of times, especially the middle-of-the-day feeding, you're running in to feed them before you run back out to do something else, and as long as you make sure the bottles are rinsed out, that's good enough."

"All right, I'll keep that in mind. If I'm going to stay on the ranch, I'd love to take over the bottle feedings."

He nodded, smiling. "I figured as much. I guess that's why I've been emphasizing not to overfeed."

"Ha. I got it. You scared me when you said it would kill them."

They walked toward the house, bottles in hand.

"I don't know if you noticed that I always keep my finger on the end on the rim of the nipple. These little guys probably won't do it, but as they get bigger, if you don't teach them to drink from a bucket, they'll be strong enough to pull the nipples off the bottle."

"You have to teach them to drink from a bucket?"

"Yeah. They'll drink water on their own, but they want to get their milk by sucking. For me, I find it just as easy to mix up a bottle as to mix up a bucket. But I suppose if you had three or more calves, buckets would make more sense, since you can really only hold two bottles at a time."

"I see. Do you think that there will be more than two?"

"Calving season is almost over, so I don't think so. But you never know. We have about twenty-five more cows to freshen before we're done."

"Freshen. That means to have their calf?"

He nodded as they walked back to the house. "That's exactly right."

She smiled to herself. Maybe she would love it here, maybe she wouldn't miss the palace at all, and maybe she would completely forget about the fact that her husband had cheated on her, if she got to stay here, and feed the calves, and listen to Baker explain things to her. He had an easygoing way about him. Although he had laughed at some of her questions, it hadn't been laughing in a mean way. It had been laughing in a way that almost made her feel like she was being funny on purpose.

Regardless, she had the feeling that she was going to love it in North Dakota.

She couldn't shake the feeling and really didn't want to as they set the bottles in by the sink and Baker showed her around the barn and outbuildings. He showed her the airplane hangar, the storage shed for the various things they needed for maintenance, the ground that had been cleared off to build some cabins for their dude ranch, and the old bunkhouse that they were going to work on fixing up. There was so much stuff going on, along with the horses and the cows and crops, and of course, Boomer followed at their heels everywhere they went.

She loved it and felt like she had fallen completely in love with the farm by the time they started strolling back to the house.

"Oh!" she said as they turned to walk back. "I didn't realize that people had shown up. That looks like Zeke's pickup."

"It does. And I think that might be Miller getting out, and maybe Elias. He was our commander in the Air Force."

"There's another car. Do you recognize that one?"

Baker didn't say anything but seemed to be studying the car as they walked closer.

The men were standing on the porch, and they'd gotten to within fifty feet of it before Baker said, "That's the preacher."

Chapter 7

Baker stared at the porch. It looked like there was going to be a conference going on in just a few minutes.

Immediately his stomach dropped. He didn't know what might have happened in town after they left, but it didn't bode well.

It also frustrated him, because he had been having such a great time with Kenni. It was like they had a connection that felt old, going way back, but was vibrant and new at the same time.

He'd never felt that with anyone else in his life before.

He'd found out today that Kenni, despite having been a princess for the last decade, was just as sweet and nice as she had been back when he knew her growing up as the girl next door. Of course, back then he'd considered her rather babyish, since she was a whole two years younger.

Until they'd kissed behind the maple tree.

That changed things forever for him.

She said he called her some other girl's name. He was positive he hadn't.

She must have misheard him, but he couldn't remember what he said.

After all, it wasn't like he'd been thinking of someone else when he was kissing her.

Regardless, he wasn't sure what the pastor was doing on their porch, but he figured it didn't bode well. And he wished there was something he could do about it. To tell the guys that if they'd just give him a little bit more time, he might have a chance with Kenni.

He had a feeling he was going to be forced into doing something that he didn't really mind, but he figured Kenni would.

"Howdy, gentlemen," he said as he hit the bottom of the stairs.

He walked up beside Kenni, who seemed to be able to tell, either from the tension that was in the air or the frowns on all of the faces that stared back at them, that something that she wasn't going to like was going down, and soon.

"So apparently you told Miss April in town today that you and Kenni are married," Zeke said, stepping forward, not paying attention to social niceties, the way good friends could often get away with.

"He had to, Zeke. The paparazzi were there. You saw them. And Miss April had her niece, who happened to be a member of the paparazzi, beside her."

Baker hid a smile. He liked the fact that Kenni had stepped forward to defend him.

He hadn't expected that, had expected her to fight her brother, not for him, but against him.

At least, if things were going the way he thought they were with the guys here. He shot another glance at the pastor, who held his Bible and another little book in his hands.

Baker clenched his jaw, so tight that he could feel it tremble and his teeth ground together.

"We already knew all that," Zeke said with a dismissive glance.

"All right, I believe it, but I don't understand why you're so upset then." She crossed her arms over her chest and stared her brother down, even though he was a good foot taller than she was.

She looked cute, and Baker tried not to grin. He had a feeling this was about to become a lot more serious, but he just had the urge to smirk.

"You lied to the whole town," Zeke said, and Baker allowed that was true. He could understand why Zeke didn't appreciate it. He wouldn't want to have to lie to support Baker's lie. Zeke didn't want to lie any more than Baker did.

But he didn't appreciate Zeke coming in so high-handed.

Some of his smirk was to hide his dismay.

He might have been able to develop something with Kenni. But these guys were going to smash whatever they had started with their high-handed techniques.

"We brought the pastor. There isn't going to be any of this fake marriage stuff going on around here. Someone has to stay with Kenni all the time, and I—"

"This is not the middle ages. I might be a woman, but I have a brain, and I'm not afraid to use it."

"No one ever said you didn't have a brain, kid."

"I'm not a kid. And it was a figure of speech."

"Whatever. Like I said, we brought the pastor and—"

"And I am not going to have you force anyone to marry me," Kenni interrupted her brother again.

"Someone has to stay with you all the time." Zeke's eyes were serious and hard, but there was also a gentleness in his tone, a gentleness that showed his love for his sister. He was truly doing what he thought was best. "If you're married to Baker, you can be with him twenty-four seven. That means people are going to expect you guys to look and act married. It really was a great idea. Not just because of that, but if people do figure out that you're Princess Kennedy, it won't matter, because once you're married to someone else, the monarchy is obviously not going to pay any ransom. So, no abductions. No lying. Brilliant." He grinned, giving her a determined look. "We're just going to make what you said today true."

"But—"

"He's right," Baker interrupted Kenni. It pained him to go against what she wanted, but he couldn't fault what Zeke had said. He hadn't considered that the abduction threat would disappear if

Kenni were to make the break from the crown completely final by marrying someone else.

He could admit to himself that if he got married to Kenni, Zeke would continue to be part of the crop dusting, and Baker assumed he would be staying home with the cows as he had been doing.

He didn't mind leaving the cows, but if he stayed home, that meant that he and Kenni would be spending time together, versus him going out with the crop-dusting crew so Zeke could stay with his sister.

"You're just going to let him railroad you into getting married?" Kenni turned around on him, and for the first time, he thought she was actually angry.

"I think he's right," Baker said simply.

"Right about what? Making you say vows you don't mean? You can't just make a mockery of marriage! If you don't mean something, you can't swear to God you're going to do it." Her voice broke on the last one, like she was so angry she could hardly stand it.

"I have every intention of keeping my vows," Baker said calmly. Her anger seemed to give him an irrational calmness. He wasn't sure where it came from, but he was thankful for it.

"You have every intention of keeping your vows? To me? Like you intend to stay married to me for the rest of your life?"

"If that's what it takes."

"What do you mean if that's what it takes? That's what you're going to be vowing."

"Then that's what I'll do."

That seemed to take the wind out of her sails. The idea that being married to her for the rest of his life wasn't a hardship. He didn't really know her, hadn't been around her for a long time, but after spending the last few hours talking and laughing with her, he knew it wouldn't be difficult to be her husband.

"If you have a problem with that, stop blaming me and speak up for yourself," he said, not wanting to but knowing that had to be where her issue lay. It wasn't that she was afraid he didn't want to stay married to her. Because that was a nonissue in his eyes. He couldn't believe how right it felt to think about pledging his life to Kenni. For her to protest, it had to be that she had bigger and better plans for her life than to be married to him.

"That's not it!" she denied immediately.

He raised a brow.

"It's not!" she denied again, her voice going slightly higher and her eyes getting big.

He lifted his shoulder like it didn't matter to him.

"You're telling me that you're going to stand here in front of the preacher, and you're going to marry me, and you're going to mean it?" she said, taking a step toward him and putting both hands on her hips while she stared him in the eyes. Somehow making it seem like she was looking down on him, like a schoolmarm on a disruptive student.

"That's exactly what I'm saying."

"Nobody asked me, but I've never seen Baker go back on his word," Elias said, just as calmly as Baker had been talking.

Baker wanted to smile, but he had a feeling that that would set Kenni off again, and he wasn't trying to make her mad on purpose. He just...just knew this was the best way. Or maybe it was exactly what he wanted.

"Someday, there might be someone you fall in love with. What are you going to do then? If you're stuck with me?"

"I'm gonna stay true to you." The answer wasn't hard.

"What about me? What if I fall in love with someone else?"

"That's you. I'm not the one who's fighting Zeke. I can see right away that it's the best thing. You're the one who's protesting."

"Fine. I won't protest." She flipped her hair back, like she was flipping her hair over her shoulder, only it was too short to even move.

He almost thought she got more frustrated, but he couldn't say for sure.

"All right. I'm ready. Let's do this thing," she said, eyeing the preacher up, who took one look at the look on her face and took a step backward.

"All right. I usually like to do a little marriage counseling before I get started," the preacher began.

"And I think marriage counseling is good, but for right now, let's get the wedding over, and then I'll make sure these two show up at your office a couple of times in the next few weeks to get a little marriage counseling. Deal?" Elias said, stepping forward and showing some emotion for the first time.

Baker tried not to laugh. Elias obviously wanted to get home in time for supper and didn't want to have to explain to his wife why he was late.

"I don't know. I kind of feel like Elias could use a little marriage counseling. Maybe we ought to call his wife and see what she says." Baker couldn't help but tease his friend.

"Are you *joking*?" Kenni said, disbelief lacing every syllable of her question.

"Not really. I just kinda feel like Jane would say that Elias could use all the help he can get. I know I feel that way."

"The feeling is mutual. Now how about you shut up so the pastor can get you hitched so I can get home for supper."

"That's what I thought," Baker said, rolling his eyes.

"If you two would join right hands."

Kenni grabbed a hold of Baker's right hand with her left.

"He said right hands," Baker said easily, reaching over and gently taking her right hand which hung at her side and lifting it up, switching out her left for her right, sliding it together slowly, carefully with his, his smooth and careful movements in direct contrast with her jerky, fast ones.

He didn't know what she thought, but he was trying to show her with his actions that he wasn't going to take this lightly. That she meant something to him, and that he would care for her and cherish her.

At his feet, Boomer whined as they stood facing each other.

No doubt the dog was jealous, unused to having to share his master.

"Hush, Boomer."

The dog was going to have to get used to it. That was good for him.

Actually, if his hunch was correct, Kenni was probably a natural with dogs, just the way she was with children. And if he wasn't careful, his dog would end up falling in love with his wife.

His *wife*.

The whole thing was surreal as the preacher said the words that Baker had heard over and over at the weddings of his friends but never thought he would hear for himself.

Or at least hadn't imagined that he would hear them today.

He certainly hadn't thought that it would be Kenni standing across from him.

He thought back to that kiss when he was seventeen. He would have married her then, fool that he was.

He had some growing up to do, and he supposed she probably did too. Not that he cared.

Still, as the pastor said the words, and he looked into her eyes, he could see the anger there, but he felt that behind the anger there was fear.

She was scared. And he couldn't blame her. It hadn't been that long since her husband had cheated on her, and she ended up divorced, out of the palace, thrown away without ceremony.

Her whole life had been twisted upside down, and then with the attempted abduction, it had been put in danger as well.

For the first time, Baker wondered if the abduction would have been people that the palace had hired to get rid of her. Maybe they were afraid she would overshadow them. Or maybe she had secrets she could tell that they didn't want to get out.

If it had been just a random stranger, Baker would assume that the threat would go away.

But if it had been a hitman hired by the royals, the threat could still be lurking out there.

He made a mental note to talk to Kenni about that later.

Of course, she might not be in any mood to talk to him later. Maybe she'd be giving him the silent treatment for a long time.

He didn't have a whole lot of experience with women, but that seemed to be one of their favorite things.

For him, sometimes it just took him a little while to think about things before he was ready to talk about them.

He'd seen other men who seemed to need to talk about things in order to think about them. Either way was okay, he supposed. He wondered which kind of person Kenni was.

"And you may kiss your bride," the pastor ended, bringing Baker's focus back to the present.

Kenni still looked angry, but she looked even more scared than she had earlier.

He wasn't going to kiss her and embarrass her in front of his friends, so he leaned over, putting his lips on her forehead and holding them there for just a second.

It was funny, since he had to fight himself to lean back.

To move away. He wanted to sit there, to breathe in her scent, to put his arms around her and hold her close. To tell her that she didn't need to be afraid, that he would give his life to save hers.

But it was hardly the time or place for all that.

Elias and Miller slapped him on the back, said a few more words to Zeke, then Elias walked down the steps, eager to get home to his own family.

The preacher stopped long enough to get his phone number so that he could set up some times for marriage counseling. "I know things are busy on the farm, and I know Kenni's situation is a little different than a normal person's, for right now anyway, being that she's trying to avoid the paparazzi, so if you need me to come out rather than you two making the trip into town, I can certainly accommodate you."

"Thanks," Baker said as he finished giving the man his number and looked at his phone to see that the pastor had texted him.

Once the pastor had walked down the stairs, and it was just Zeke and Kenni and him on the porch, Zeke said, "Sorry about that, Kenni, but it really is the best way."

"I guess I just don't see it. We're not living in the dark ages. We don't *have* to get married anymore."

"It wasn't a matter of you *having* to get married. It was a matter of protection."

"I don't understand why you didn't think that you could protect me."

"You being married is going to protect you. It was a brilliant idea. But it has to be real. It can't be something that you guys are just saying, with no substance behind it." He let out a frustrated breath. "I know lying is something everyone does nowadays, but I know it has to grate on you and on Baker, and I hate it too. Lying isn't the answer."

Baker figured she understood, just didn't like it, but she pressed her mouth closed, crossing her arms over her chest and looking off toward where the sun was setting in the distance.

"You mind if I carry your things in?"

"No, that's fine," she said, not bothering to look back over her shoulder at him while she spoke.

"I never showed her around the house. She didn't have any of her things, and it was time for me to feed the calves." Baker started toward the steps. His stomach rumbled. "She's probably hungry too."

"Well, you're the husband. You better feed her." Zeke smirked at him, truly smiling for the first time since Baker had stepped up on the porch, before he turned around and walked in the house.

Baker looked over at Kenni. At his wife. What a mess.

Chapter 8

"So, um, we have hot dogs," Baker said, and Kenni wasn't sure whether she should laugh or cry.

She was married. Newly *married*.

She had sworn she would never get married again. One cheating husband was enough cheating husbands for a lifetime.

Of course, Baker wasn't anything like Isaac, but still. She didn't want to get married.

And yet, she hadn't really protested. She'd...allowed them to... Had they pushed her? Or had she walked willingly?

Maybe because it was Baker. Maybe because of her long-ago crush, of how she looked up to him, admired him, and respected him. How she knew he was a man of character who would do what he said he would do.

"I'm hungry," she said. If they had hot dogs, that's what she'd eat.

"I know you're used to something better." Baker ran a hand through his hair.

"It's okay. That's what you have, that's what we'll eat."

"It's not a very good wedding meal."

"Baker," she said, waiting until his eyes raised to meet hers. "It's fine."

"What's fine? The hot dogs? Or the wedding?"

"Both. We're going to make both work." She lifted her chin; maybe it was a little bit of a challenge. "Isn't that what life is? Taking what you get and making the best of it? Does it really matter what you have? I mean, we always think it does. We always look around and think, oh, if I had that, or if I had this, or if I had servants, or if I didn't have to cook, or if I didn't live here."

She shrugged her shoulders and lifted her hands, indicating the farm, the area they were, all of North Dakota, she didn't know.

"It just doesn't matter. I can live in a palace and have servants waiting on me hand and foot and still not be happy. It... It's more important that I just choose to make the best with what I have."

Even if it was a cheating husband. Or if it was an unexpected marriage she still wasn't sure about.

In life, she didn't get to turn back time, she had to keep walking. Keep trying to learn from the mistakes she made and not make the same mistakes again. To do the best with the time that God had given her.

"God gives us free choice. We don't get to choose when we're born, we don't get to choose when we die, but we do get to choose whether or not we're going to be happy between the two appointed times, and we do get to choose whether or not we're going to be profitable with our life or waste it on things that really don't matter."

"Like complaining about what's for supper?"

"Sure. Or..." She thought of Isaac. His main goal in life was to get through his royal duties so that he could watch rugby on TV or play rugby or attend games. It was what he lived for.

Maybe it was best that he had cheated on her, because the longer she spent with him, the more she thought that type of existence was a waste.

She had thrown herself into her royal duties, trying to do her very best, trying to bring attention to the causes that really needed help. Rather than wasting her time on whining about freedoms or whatever she didn't have, or just putting her time in, and only really concerned about making herself happy, whether by shopping, or going out with friends, or swimming in the palace pool. Not that she didn't do all of those activities, there was nothing wrong with them in general, but having fun couldn't be her focus.

"Or what?" Baker prompted when she forgot that she was even talking.

"Or complaining about the jobs we have. The work we do. Why not focus on making our work meaningful? On making our lives count? Instead of doing our best to rush through our lives so we can get to what we consider the 'good' parts. The parts where we're entertaining ourselves, or playing, or doing what we consider 'fun.'"

He looked at her like he'd never seen her before. "That's something you learned at the palace?"

She nodded. "At first, I hated the duties I had. I hated having every day scheduled down to the minute, but...I had a unique position, an ability to do something no one else in the world could. An ability to help people focus their attention on causes that were good for mankind. I realized—it took me longer than it should have—that me resenting my place was foolish. I should take the opportunities I had and invest my time wisely on things bigger than myself."

"That's smart."

She smiled a little. "This isn't exactly a palace, but it's the same thing, isn't it? Sometimes life happens, and we resent the situations we find ourselves in, instead of looking at the situation trying to figure out how we can turn it into a blessing. Not just for ourselves, but for others. Or even if we don't resent our lives, we forget that that life that we have is a gift—we can use it wisely, or we can waste it on ourselves."

"I didn't really have any doubts about our wedding, but you're really making me feel like marrying you was probably the best decision I've ever made."

She liked that, mostly. Although, she supposed every woman wanted a husband who loved her. One who admired her and respected her, not just her intellect and the things that she did, but her as a person.

Of course, she supposed if she had a choice, she would rather her husband admire her intellect and accomplishments than her looks.

"So do I cook the hot dogs? Or do you?"

"Are you asking who's going to be the cook in this relationship?" he asked with a grin, and she got the feeling that he didn't really care. Whether she could cook, whether she couldn't, whether she wanted to, or whether she didn't. Or maybe he was just confident that she would do whatever needed to be done, whether it was work she wanted to do or work she didn't.

"Well, if hot dogs are your specialty, and since I'm feeling like I'm probably going to end up being the one to spend the majority of the time in the kitchen, I can do it. However, if you want to give me a break every once a while and cook hot dogs for supper, that's fine."

"Oh, I can do more than hot dogs. I'm actually really good at opening up cans, and I can make chicken noodle soup really fast. The only problem is we don't have any right now."

"Oh. Inhibited by a lack of ingredients, not talent."

"Exactly."

"I'll keep that in mind."

"Do you want me to give you a tour of the house before I cook the hot dogs?"

"I suppose that would be a good idea. I...don't think there are too many people who have gotten married on the front porch before they even stepped into the house."

"I'm sorry about that."

"No. Don't be. I'm imagining that it will be a fun story to tell twenty years from now."

"Is it really going to take twenty years to turn that into fun?"

"Tomorrow might be a little bit soon. But next year?"

"I'll ask you then."

She walked in, loving the way he smiled at her and wondering if it was going to be possible for her to be married to him and not fall in love with him. After all, she smiled more in the last six hours than she smiled in a very long time. Of course, everyone always said rebound relationships didn't work.

And despite the fact that her marriage ended a while ago, this was her first relationship since then.

And marriage.

It would work if they both decided they were going to do everything in their power to make it work.

"There are four bedrooms upstairs. Zeke and Miller each have one, and I have the third. Gideon moved out of the fourth, so you can either have his one or...you can share mine."

Her breath caught. She hadn't even really thought of that. Her steps slowed as she climbed, her hand gripping the banister.

What should she do?

He was obviously leaving it up to her. But she didn't have a clue.

"Can I look at the bedrooms?" she asked, maybe just to stall more than because she wanted to see them.

"Of course. Mine is the smallest room. Actually, I chose first and picked the smallest one on purpose, just because I didn't really care and didn't plan to spend any more time in my bedroom than it took to sleep at night."

"I see. That was smart."

"Yeah. And the bedroom that's left would be the closest bedroom to the bathroom. So I can understand why you might want it."

"Okay, so that's the bathroom right there." She pointed to the door that hung open, exposing a bit of a white linoleum.

"Right. And the empty bedroom is right here." He pushed the door next to the bathroom open.

"I love these windows," she said, looking at the afternoon sunbeams as they slanted across the room and hit the floor.

"It helps keep it warm in the winter," Baker said, not really giving a clue as to what he wanted her to do. "The other three bedrooms are down there. They are smaller, with mine being, like I said, the smallest."

"If you don't mind, I think I'll take this one." Her voice sounded a little breathy, because she intended to say a little bit more. "I... I assume that we both meant for this to be a real marriage. We talked about keeping our marriage vows until death parts us. But the fact that we just met each other again after ten years probably means that we might want to get to know each other a little bit?"

She didn't add "at first," or "before we did anything," or whatever it was that she should say. But he didn't need her to explain what she meant. He understood.

"Again, that's fine. I'm sure we'll be sharing a room at some point, so you can just let me know when you want me to move. Will that work?"

He handled that so casually that she almost forgot to be embarrassed. In fact, she wasn't. Not at all.

"That sounds fine. Or if you feel like it might be time and I'm not thinking about it or haven't said anything, you can say something, too."

"All right. I'll do that, but I'll probably leave it up to you. Unless it takes longer than it takes for you to laugh about getting married on the porch of the house you're going to live in before you set foot in it."

"Fair enough. I usually adjust pretty quickly, but I don't know." Physical intimacy was a little bit different than learning to laugh. Being comfortable with someone she barely knew or being attracted to them, or... She wasn't even sure. In a marriage like theirs, where they got married without really considering attraction or even whether or not they liked each other, how did one tell when one was ready to share a room?

She was pretty sure there weren't too many people handing out advice on a situation like that, since it wasn't a situation that typically cropped up in modern times.

Well, she'd just have to pray about it and take her cues from the Lord. He would help her if she asked.

"Is this everything?" Baker said, indicating her luggage, as they started back down the steps. They were old and creaking, and several of them felt loose underneath her feet.

"I don't have that much."

"You moved out of a castle, and you don't have much stuff?"

"Well, I didn't have a lot of time to pack. But also, as I looked at my wardrobes, and yes, I had more than one, full of clothes, I realized that a lot of them weren't mine. They were just loaned to me by different designers, hoping I would showcase their work. And I did," she said easily, as they hit the bottom of the stairs and Baker nodded toward a room.

"Living room."

"I see."

"So you left all the clothes there?"

"The ones that weren't mine. I really didn't know where I'd wear them anyway. It wasn't like I was planning on going and being high society. I'm just...just a small-town girl from the South. I don't have fancy places to go. Or anywhere to wear clothes like I had in Corinth."

"I see. You don't really sound sad about that."

"I told you it was hard for me to adjust to palace life at first. Going places where people expected you to have your clothes and your hair and your makeup perfect all the time was one of those adjustments that were hard for me."

"So it's not something you'll miss."

"Probably not. For the most part, no."

"This is the kitchen. There's no dining room, but you can see it's pretty big and we have a table in here."

"Nice. This is one of the places you renovated?"

"It is."

"I thought I smelled fresh-cut wood."

"Yeah, I made the table. That's probably what you smell, although the cabinets are new too, and we put the tile down, but obviously that doesn't smell like fresh-cut wood."

She laughed a little. "I like the table. It's big and looks solid."

"Yeah. We can butcher a deer on here, or an elk, or have a Thanksgiving feast. It's built to handle whatever a farm family needs."

Chapter 9

Kenni pressed her lips together, tilting her head and looking at Baker. It almost sounded like when he made the table, he had some dreams of his own. Of a big farm family, of a happy life. Of people working together and sharing chores to make everything easier. Of laughter and fun. Of work and play.

Of course, he didn't articulate all of that, and she didn't expect him to, but she felt like it was there. Just a glimmer of it. Maybe not even to the point where he thought in words about it, just where he had some hopes of his own.

Not that she didn't expect him to, but the idea surprised her.

In a good way.

"You put some thought into that," she said.

"I guess I did. Of course, when I made it, I never pictured you standing here beside me, thinking that it would be ours."

"I'm sure you didn't." She had been on the other side of the world, dealing with a marriage that was crumbling and expectations that felt too heavy for one person to bear.

He stood in the kitchen, staring at the table, and he seemed to be rolling something over in his head. She wasn't in any rush to do anything, but her stomach did growl, reminding her that it had been a long day. Finally, he rapped his knuckles on the table and then turned to her.

"Do you think you can be happy here?"

She blinked. The question had taken her by surprise. They'd talked about choosing happiness and her belief that it was within a person's ability to decide how their life was going to turn out, for the most part. Sure, there were things they couldn't choose, birth, death, even sickness and disease to some extent, but...happiness was a choice.

She didn't wait too long but faced him fully, her shoulders back. "Yes. Yes, I can. I'm looking forward to our life. Looking forward to what God has planned for me. The doors He's going to open, the things you and I will do together."

"You're used to having lots of things. A big life. Lots of people looking at you. Lots of influence, like you said earlier. There's none of that here. There's no glory, no cameras, other than the ones we're running from."

She laughed at that.

He kept talking. "No recognition. Just a lot of work. Long days, long nights in the winter. A lot of cold and endless wind. It's a hard life."

His eyes scrunched up a little, and he looked at her, almost like he was sorry for dragging her into it.

"You were just looking to get away. And now here you are, with a life you weren't expecting, and...I don't think you realize how hard it's going to be."

"I like a challenge."

"This is a challenge that goes on and on and on. There's really not ever a time where you're going to feel like, okay. I won. There are just little battles. Ones you win or lose on a daily basis. Sometimes big battles."

"All right. Bring it on," she said, and maybe she was overconfident.

Maybe she really didn't realize how hard it was going to be. Maybe he was right.

But then again, maybe he underestimated her. Maybe he didn't realize that sure, life in the palace had been cushy in a lot of ways, but it had been extremely difficult in a lot of other ways. A lot of people would have given up. Would have walked away. Would have not been able to stand the pressure, to handle the expectations, to submit to the things that they needed to do in order to thrive like she had in the institution and help it continue to have the influence it had for centuries.

She had to come to a point where she realized that what she did was greater than herself. Greater than making herself look good, greater than putting herself first.

It had been an exercise in humility. An exercise in putting others first. An exercise in realizing that she was just a small part on the world stage, but she had learned to use her influence as wisely as she could. Not for herself, but for others.

This would be different. Of course. But the general lessons would be the same. That life was not about her. That she would learn to do the work she had to do without thought to herself.

She felt a touch on her shoulder, and she looked down to see Baker's fingers sliding around, holding on, gently but firmly.

"I don't want this to beat you down. This land, it can be hard. And I love the spirit that you're showing. The attitude, the grit and determination. I don't want you to lose that."

She looked for another moment at his fingers, then her hand came up, and she put her fingers over top of his. They threaded together, and she lifted his hand to her mouth, bringing his first finger to her lips and pressing them against it.

"Isn't everything easier with two people?" she asked softly, look-ing at him.

He huffed out a breath, a little laugh maybe. But one of his lips pulled back. "I think it depends on whether those two people are pulling in the same direction or not, doesn't it?"

He had a point.

She smiled a small smile, nodding. "Then we just have to make sure that we're working for the same things, right?"

"Guess that's what being married is. Two people, learning to be one."

It was her turn to pull her lips back and look away. She'd been married once. She thought she tried as hard as she could to fit into the institution that Isaac was a part of. To throw herself into doing what she was supposed to do as his wife. Into supporting him, as a future king. But she had been alone. She had probably been more alone in the decade of her marriage than she had been in all of her life.

"It's lonely when you're in a marriage by yourself," she finally said, knowing that wasn't really what he meant, but that had been her experience. She and Isaac hadn't been pulling for an same things all the time. He had been supporting the monarchy, of course, but he hadn't really been interested in strengthening their marriage.

"Why did he marry you?" Baker asked, almost as though the thought had just occurred to him.

She shrugged. "I've asked myself that over and over. I guess we had a whirlwind courtship, and the sensationalism of Isaac choosing, not just an American, but a commoner. Someone he met on the train of all places. Maybe we were just both swept into the idea that it would be good for the American press to be involved. And I think our marriage and relationship was good for the country of Corinth."

"You paid a high price."

She nodded slowly. She was still paying the price. She probably always would be paying the price. There would be those memories. Those what ifs. Those areas where she had sore spots, scars, baggage that stemmed from her time in the palace.

She didn't want that to define her life though.

"I guess I paid. I'm still paying. But again, I learned a lot. An awful lot. I grew up. I learned that I can do things I didn't think I could do. I saw a lot of the world and had experiences I would never have had without it."

"Sounds a lot like my experience with the Air Force."

"It was hard?" she asked, surprised.

"No. Just...it grew me. Gave me experiences I wouldn't have had otherwise. I learned a lot. I saw some of the world. And I learned to do things I didn't think I could do. I... I don't know that I would do it again if I have the choice."

"Same."

That was the honest truth. While she could focus on the good and determine that she would use that experience to her advantage, it didn't necessarily mean that she wanted to repeat it. Or that she didn't consider it a mistake.

They smiled at each other. Understanding seemed to flow between them. Both of them seemed to know what the other was thinking, and she wasn't sure she ever felt that with anyone else. Her experience in the palace had been unique, in her eyes anyway, but there were definitely things that other people could understand.

Baker had made the effort to try to understand her.

"Thank you," she said, squeezing his hand.

His fingers wrapped and twisted around hers, until their clasped hands dangled between them. "For what?"

"For taking the time to talk to me."

"Isn't that what a husband is supposed to do?"

"Just because a husband is supposed to do it doesn't mean he does." Oh, that was so very true. She had lived it.

"I suppose the same is true for a wife?"

"I sure hope not this wife," she said, more feeling in her words than maybe the statement warranted. But it was the truth. She didn't want to be the kind of wife who didn't care about being the best that she could be. Who didn't try to treat her husband with love and respect and do everything she could to make his life better because he'd pledged it to hers.

"All right then. Let's get some food into you. Because I'm pretty sure that's my job tonight." He smiled and she returned it, loving the foundation they were building together.

They had easy camaraderie as they cooked the hot dogs together.

Zeke and Miller joined them later, and they ate together.

She retired before any of the men, and if Miller or Zeke said anything about her going to a separate room, she didn't hear it.

Maybe Baker understood that only knowing someone for one day wasn't nearly long enough, or maybe he thought it was.

Regardless, Baker had handled that aspect of their relationship as well as she could possibly have hoped.

After she had showered, she stood at the window, looking at the clear North Dakota sky. All the stars twinkling, no moon in sight.

This would be her view. It could be her view for the rest of her life.

She thought about the years passing, about the things that could happen to them. Probably things she could never imagine, hopes and dreams, happiness and sorrows. Holidays and friends, and a lot of work. He'd warned her.

Lord, I want to do my best in the life You've given me. Please help me.

Whatever the future held, she wanted to face it with grace and integrity. With courage and strength. Whether she left a legacy that millions of people would see, or whether she left a legacy that only the town of Sweet Water might remember. She wanted to leave a path that other people could follow, footsteps that showed the way for others.

If even one person could be guided to a life of service to the Lord, then she would consider her life a success.

Chapter 10

Kenni hadn't considered what time she might need to get up in the morning, but when she rolled out of bed at seven o'clock, the house was quiet.

She didn't hear anything as she got dressed and walked to the bathroom, and still nothing when she walked downstairs.

The kitchen was empty, the coffeepot cold.

She pulled out her phone but then realized that she hadn't gotten Baker's number.

She laughed out loud in the quiet kitchen. She didn't even have her husband's phone number.

What kind of modern woman was she?

But she did have Zeke's, so she texted her brother, even though she felt like an idiot because she had to ask her brother for her husband's phone number.

She figured she could have just asked Zeke if they had had breakfast, or if they wanted her to cook it.

Walking to the refrigerator, she opened it up and saw that there were eggs in a bowl, not in an egg carton.

She thought she remembered something about chickens, from the day before. She had seen them, and he pointed out the coop, but she couldn't remember what he had said about the eggs.

And she wanted to know if he had fed the calves. Should she do that? He'd shown her how but hadn't said that it would be her responsibility.

She should have talked to him about the things that were important, instead of talking about her past experiences.

That hadn't solved any problems, and although she felt a tighter bond with Baker today than she did yesterday, it hadn't helped her figure out what in the world she was supposed to do.

Other than lie low and not blow her cover. As for working on the farm...she didn't know what her jobs entailed.

Funny how the world of Corinth, the palace and all of the fancy things that constantly surrounded her, as well as her strictly scheduled days, seemed like a lifetime ago.

Her phone buzzed, and she looked down to read Zeke's text.

I forgot to tell you the old coots are coming to film a TikTok video on the farm today.

No number; he didn't answer her question.
She texted back.

All right. What time?

If that's what he wanted to talk about, that was what she'd talk about.

I don't know.

Do you have Baker's number?

Listen, I can't be your marriage counselor.

I'm asking for his number, not advice on what to do in my marriage!

Big brothers could be so annoying.

Give me a minute. I'm busy. I'll send it when I have two hands.

Okay. That was a better excuse.
She decided she'd walk outside and see what kind of day it was.

She opened the door but hadn't gotten one foot outside when something ran past her, startling her so that she jumped. "Oh!"

She looked down to see a cat running through the doorway and onto the porch.

Baker had specifically said the cats were indoor cats, so she pushed the door open and hurried out. But the cat ran from her, scurrying off the porch and squeezing through a crack underneath it.

That was wonderful. Her first day on the farm, and she would lose their beloved cats.

Neither one of the cats had come out to welcome her yesterday. Baker had said that they were usually skittish around strangers, but they'd warm up to her. He talked about them with affection, and she figured they must love them to have kept them on despite the fact that they'd gotten them to eat mice and they didn't.

She didn't know how long the warm-up period would be before they decided they liked her, but she would definitely be more careful when she opened the door. She didn't want the cats to run away because she had moved in.

She was on her hands and knees, trying to use her phone flashlight to see through the crack, calling, "Here, kitty, kitty," when the sound of a motor startled her.

She turned around to see a big SUV pulling up.

It was a little embarrassing to be caught on her hands and knees looking under the porch, but surely she wasn't the only person who had ever lost a cat outside.

Just as she was starting to push up, she saw a nose at the opening.

Torn between whether she needed to greet her guests or continue trying to get the cat, she looked toward the vehicle, where Gideon, one of her brother's buddies, got out on one side and a woman she didn't recognize got out of the other.

It must be Gideon's wife, although she hadn't met her yet. What was her name?

Piper. She was pretty sure her name was Piper.

"Hey there. Is there a problem?" Gideon's smile faded as he took in her position while she stared at him.

"I'm sorry. I lost a cat. It's under there. I just saw its nose."

"I've actually not seen the cats since I moved out. They're shy with strangers."

"Yeah. This one won't come to me. I don't even know which one it is."

"I can give you a hand. I seem to have a thing about cats and kids. They're attracted to me," Piper said as she hurried over, kneeling down beside Kenni.

"I'd appreciate it. I'd really hate to lose a cat on my first day on the farm. It doesn't really bode well for a good start."

"I'll say."

"So...you lose cats. How do you do with kids?" Gideon asked, sounding uncertain.

"Um, I've never lost a child," she said, shrugging, unsure what that had to do with anything, but feeling like she needed to be completely honest. "I've never really watched any for any length of time. Not all by myself."

"Oh. Well, Piper's mom called, and her dad had to be rushed to the hospital. We didn't want her to be at the hospital by herself, but we didn't want to take all of the kids with us either."

"Are they in school?" Kenni asked, eyeing Piper as she put her fingers on the ground, tapping them gently and calling softly. A feline face appeared.

"No. Summer vacation."

"Oh yeah. Of course."

"I... The older kids can take care of themselves, but the two little ones will definitely need supervision, although not constant attention."

"I'm so sorry about your dad," Kenni said, her brain working slowly as she watched Piper easily get the cat to come to her. Soon, she was holding it in her arms.

"It's okay. I'm more concerned about my mom. My dad always takes things in stride, but Mom panics. She probably needs someone there to help her stay calm, and if there's any decisions to be made, she'll be pretty much worthless."

"All right. I'm...I'm happy to watch the kids. But...I'm honestly probably not going to be any better with them than I am with cats."

"It's really not hard. As long as you feed them, they'll be happy. Just make sure they don't do anything that will hurt anything on the farm or themselves. The older four will be a help if you want them. The younger will want to help, but like I said, you'll have to keep an eye on them."

"I can do it."

She didn't know what else she was going to have to do that day, but she knew that Gideon was one of Baker's best friends, and she wasn't going to turn down his request for help. Obviously, he came here thinking that he could depend on his friends to give him a hand. She didn't want to be the one who turned him away. And she couldn't imagine Baker not lending a hand if he could.

"By the way, I'm Piper. Gideon told me about you and Baker getting married yesterday, but I had the kids, so I didn't make a meal or anything, and now with my parents..."

"Nice to meet you," Kenni said, taking Piper's hand. And liking her immediately. She seemed friendly and down to earth. With no guile and no snobbery. Just a very real, very kind person.

"We'll definitely be back tonight. No matter what shape my dad is in, we're not going to just leave you indefinitely with our children."

"Do what you need to do, and I'll do my best with the kids. If you give me the cat, I'll take it inside, and then you can introduce me to them." She laughed a little. "I'd introduce you to the cat, but I honestly have no idea what its name is."

She felt like an outsider in her own home.

Of course, it was a little early for her to feel right at home. After all, she'd barely been there twelve hours.

Gideon and Piper were back at their car getting their kids out after she put the cat in, admonishing it to stay inside where it belonged.

"I know six kids is a lot, so I told them that they need to help you with their names, because it can be a little confusing. We didn't use any kind of rhyme or reason when we named them," Piper said with a small, apologetic shrug of her shoulders.

"This is Lucas. He's the oldest, and he'll be a good help to you. Just tell him what to do, and he'll do it. He's my right-hand man at home," Gideon introduced his oldest son. "And this is Alice. She's the same. We couldn't run the house without her. She's a great mom to the younger ones. She'll definitely give you a hand with them."

Gideon smiled with pride at his children, and Kenni's heart turned over.

She'd been disappointed when she and Isaac hadn't had children, but as things got worse and worse in their marriage, the less chance there was of kids happening, and the more she felt like it might have been a good thing.

Eventually they would have had to address the concerns about an heir to the throne, but considering that they had another fifteen years of childbearing or so, no one had been in any rush.

They introduced the other four children, Ingrid, the middle child, then Henry, Luna, and Theodora, who was two.

"Let me give you my cell phone number in case you need it. I know Baker will help you. Jonah, I'm not sure if you met him or not, but I know he and Darby will give you a hand as well. And of course, Zeke and Miller."

"Isn't one of them out on a crop-dusting run?" Kenni asked hesitantly. She had heard something to that effect yesterday.

"I think it's just a day trip. They're not far away," Gideon said, nodding his head.

"All right," Kenni said, trying to infuse confidence in her smile when she felt anything but.

In fact, she felt rather overwhelmed with the children, although Alice already had Theodora in her arms while Luna held onto her leg.

Lucas stood with Ingrid and Henry, his hand on either one of their shoulders, almost as though assuring them that everything would be okay.

"All right, we'll let Miss Kenni know if there are any issues, and we should be back before supper." Gideon looked at the children, and they nodded, Lucas and Alice looking competent, but the other ones in various stages of distress. Except for Theodora, who seemed perfectly content to suck her thumb and hold onto Alice.

They stood and watched while their parents got in the SUV and drove away.

Kenni checked her phone, just in case Zeke had sent Baker's number. But he hadn't.

She could only hope that Baker would ask Zeke for hers. Then she laughed. Maybe he had and Zeke had done the whole stonewalling thing to him as well.

Regardless, she had children to feed now.

"Did you guys have any breakfast?"

"No. But I can help make it," Alice said, her look eager.

"All right. I'll take you up on that." She gave Alice a smile, thinking about what a blessing she must be to her mom. "All right. If you guys will follow me, we'll go inside. Be careful with the door, because I already lost the cat once this morning."

"Cats like me," the middle child, Ingrid, said. "If she runs out, I can catch her for you." Her little hand slipped into Kenni's, and something squeezed around Kenni's heart.

Yes. She definitely wanted children.

She'd have to talk to Baker about that...maybe not soon. But sometime.

The kids chattered as they went in, Kenni watching the door to make sure the cat didn't escape again, and she showed them to the kitchen.

Her phone buzzed in her pocket, and she almost gave an audible sigh of relief, taking it out and expecting to see a text from Baker.

It was her brother again.

> **Baker said to tell you that some dude just texted him and is on his way with a goat he found on the road. He said we could put it in the side pen for now. The man said it was pregnant.**

She ground her teeth together, her thumbs hitting her phone screen with short, angry taps.

> **Did you tell Baker I wanted his number?**

> **Forgot.**

> **I just reminded you. I need to talk to my husband.**

She didn't figure there was any point in telling Zeke about the kids. He'd just get a big kick out of that.

As she went to the kitchen, her eye caught a movement out the window, and she realized it was a pickup coming in the drive.

"Okay, guys. I know I said we were going to eat, but I think this man might be bringing us a goat. We need to go out and make sure it gets put in the side pen."

"Goat? Can we pet it?" Ingrid said excitedly, while even Lucas, with his more serious expression, had a smile on his face.

"I'm sure we probably can. Although, I don't know anything about it. We'll ask."

She had no idea whether goats were safe to pet. But they were small, and as long as it didn't have horns... Did all goats have horns?

Funny the facts she needed to recall as she lived her daily life. Usually they were not things she had actually learned in school on purpose.

The kids filed back out of the kitchen, with Henry running and jumping and Lucas telling him to stop.

She figured it was probably hard for a little fella to be as serious as his older siblings wanted him to be, and she made a note that when they got outside, Lucas could allow Henry to run around. There wasn't too much he could get hurt on, as long as he didn't cross any fences and get lost in any pastures.

Unfortunately, as the door opened again, she saw the now familiar blur of movement, and the same cat that had gone out earlier zipped outside again.

"Oh, no! The cat's out!"

Now she had kids and needed to keep track of them while once again needing to get a cat back in the house.

"Watch where it goes!"

"It went under the porch," Alice said, leaning over the banister and pointing to the same hole that Piper had just gotten it out of.

"Cats like me! I can get it!" Ingrid said as the pickup pulled to a stop just behind Baker's truck.

"All right. If you do that, can you put it back in the house when you're done?"

"Can I cuddle it some?"

"Sure, you can. Just don't go anywhere so I can find you," Kenni said, not remembering her mom ever giving her directions like that but not knowing what else to say. It was one thing to lose a cat. It was a completely different story to lose a kid.

> Hey! Zeke finally gave me your number. Sorry I forgot to ask you for it. There's supposed to be a thunderstorm coming in an hour or so. Can you make sure all the plastic out by the barn has something sitting on it so it doesn't blow away?

She finally got a text from her husband.

She kept walking, making sure that the two little kids were still with Alice and Lucas as they headed toward the pickup. Her thumbs flew over the buttons on her phone.

Sure. Did you feed the calves?

No. I thought you wanted to?

I will. I just didn't know.

She had to remember how to do it. Of course the kids would help her, but it would be her first time doing it on her own, and she didn't know whether she was competent enough to do it herself, let alone give instructions to the kids on how to do it.

Regardless, she swallowed that fear down and figured that she'd have to wait to feed the kids until she fed the calves. Or should she feed the kids first?

She tried to set those thoughts aside and focus on the scene in front of her.

"I don't usually pick animals up from the side of the road, but she was going to get hit," the man drawled slowly as he slammed the door of his pickup shut and walked around the other side.

He had the goat in the front seat of his truck?

"All right. I am Kenni, by the way."

"Heard you married Baker," the man said over his shoulder as he strolled around the front of the truck. His movements, his words, his steps, nothing about him was fast, but it was still a shorter time than Kenni was ready for before he had pulled the goat out of the front seat of his truck by the horns.

So, she did have horns. Great. Were they dangerous?

She'd Google it as soon as she had a minute.

"I need you to put her in the pen by the barn."

"No. I just said I was going to drop her off. She's not mine." He gave a little grin, slow like the rest of him. "She's your goat now."

"All right." She took a deep breath. She could handle this.

"She's got feet sticking out."

Chapter 11

Feet sticking out?

"Excuse me?" Kenni asked, unsure exactly what that meant. Was it some kind of colloquialism that she wasn't familiar with?

"She's having a baby. Take her where you want them to be born. You probably have maybe five minutes. Tops." The man grinned again, looked at her for a second, then turned his head and spit. He wiped his mouth with the back of his hand, then slapped one hand down on the hood of his pickup. "I need to get home afore the storm. I've got me some stuff what needs tied down. Supposed to be a barnburner."

Barnburner? Was he talking about the storm? Did that mean a bad storm or a good storm?

She wasn't exactly sure, but she wiped the sweat from where it dripped down her temple with the back of her hand, and she wasn't quite sure where the urge came from, but she wanted to turn her head and spit too.

Peer pressure probably.

Or the effects of unmitigated stress.

Regardless, she swallowed the urge to spit and stared at the goat. It had four feet. There was nothing weird about that. Whatever the man had meant, obviously it wasn't anything she needed to worry about.

However, the idea that she was having a baby was definitely something that concerned her. Five minutes. She had five minutes. Maybe four by now.

Somewhere she had heard that she wasn't supposed to pull a goat by its horns. She couldn't remember where, and she didn't see any other way of leading the animal, but if the man was right and the goat was having a baby, they needed to get her somewhere and fast.

"I see the feet he was talking about," Alice said, and Kenni looked at her.

"The feet?"

"The baby's feet are sticking out," Alice said, biting her lip and looking at Kenni like Kenni could somehow do something about that.

Something other than panic.

She really, really felt like panicking. Funny how a person got into a situation like this, and panic seemed like a logical and productive way to spend time.

She swallowed. Her throat was dry.

The man had walked to his pickup, and the sound of the motor turning over filled the air along with blue smoke from his exhaust as he backed out.

"All right. We have feet. That's great. Has anyone here ever delivered babies before?"

Any kind of baby. Even a cow baby would probably be helpful in this situation. Wouldn't it? Did cows and goats have babies the same way?

"I heard Dad say that babies usually didn't need help. It's just if the mom is having problems. He said you usually just stand back and watch, and God equipped them to do what needed to be done."

Kenni looked down, staring at Lucas, wondering if that was advice she could use.

It sounded reasonable. After all, most babies were born with no problem, right?

She had no idea.

"All right. So let's stand back."

"I thought we were supposed to put it in a pen?" Henry asked, tilting his head at the goat, like he was trying to figure out if she would fit in a pen.

"I think… Maybe we'll just let her have her baby here. I'm not sure how to lead her anyway, and I'm not sure if we move her whether that's going to be good for her or not?"

"I caught the cat!" Ingrid yelled from by the porch.

"Thank you. That's great. Can you put it in the house, please?" Her tone was distracted, and she didn't even take the time to be happy that she didn't lose her husband's cat on their first day of marriage.

Before she could say anything else, a car passed the pickup which was rolling slowly up the lane. She certainly wasn't surprised that the pickup was going slowly. That man didn't seem to have a fast bone in his body, but the car that was coming was certainly flying.

It didn't exactly screech to a halt where the pickup had just been parked, but it did leave about four inches of skid marks on the stone driveway.

A rather frazzled woman jumped out of the car and ran around to the passenger side of the car.

She waved her hand in the air in a frenzied but friendly greeting. "Hi! I'm Darby. Sorry I can't stop to introduce myself. I was hoping I could use an electrical outlet?"

"What?" Kenni said.

Ever since she'd gotten out of bed that morning, she felt like she was running about six steps behind everyone else, and she had a feeling that nothing was going to change in the next ten minutes.

"An electrical outlet," the woman yelled as she opened the back door of her car and pulled out a box.

She grabbed something else, something metal with a cord, and then shut the door with her hip.

"Um, sure?" Kenni said as the woman hurried by her.

"Thank you!" the woman called over her shoulder, continuing her mad dash for the house. "I just got chicks, and my last batch, all twenty-five of them, died when I left the house and the heat light burned out. I'm not going to allow that to happen to these little guys. Not on your life," she said as the screen door slammed behind her but not before the cat ran out again.

Maybe the cat should be an outside cat. It appeared to like the outdoors much better than the indoors.

"Ingrid?" she asked, hoping that was the name of the kid that was able to get the cat out from underneath the porch before. She was having trouble keeping her life straight at the moment.

"Yes, ma'am? I wanted to see the baby goat be born. So I put the cat inside."

"That's fine. Do you, um, do you think you might be able to get the cat out quickly?"

"I don't know. It took a long time last time."

"I see a nose!" Alice said, from her vantage point behind the goat.

Was it okay for a two-year-old to watch a goat be born? She wasn't sure. She couldn't think of anything that would be wrong with that. So she didn't say anything about Alice holding Luna and Lucas holding Theodora, all of them standing back watching the goat as she grunted, hunched up, and pushed.

Should she help with the goat or the cat? Or should she go inside and offer her guest refreshments?

That's what she would do if she were in the palace.

Of course she wouldn't have someone dropping in without being on the schedule. And she certainly wouldn't have someone dropping in carrying a cardboard box full of... Did she say chicks?

She was pretty sure she said chicks. Did she mean baby chickens?

The box wasn't big enough to hold full-grown chickens.

A calf bawled, reminding Kenni that she hadn't fed them yet. And Baker had said he usually fed them as soon as he got up in the morning.

They were probably at least two hours overdue for their bottles.

And he had been very careful to feed them on time, because he wanted to feed them three or four times a day.

"Baaa!"

She turned around quickly. The goat sounded like it was in distress.

"I think the baby is stuck!"

Before Kenni could say anything, another car pulled into the driveway.

She supposed it was too much to ask for this car to actually be bringing her some help, instead of another catastrophe.

She thought she saw two bald heads in the front, older gentlemen, the old coots Zeke had mentioned in his text, maybe? Another head bopped around in the back seat.

Maybe these were the people who were going to be making a TikTok video?

Actually, that's probably what Darby was going to do. Didn't Baker say something about Darby and the old coots?

Why were they doing it on the farm again? She couldn't remember. Except technically, Darby lived on the farm, just over in the big farmhouse.

The goat baaed again, and Kenni was pretty sure she heard the calf bawl as well.

She needed to do this. She really wanted to be able to handle things. To be a good farm wife, but she was feeling more than a little overwhelmed. She pulled her phone out of her pocket, needing Baker to come help her. This was way more than she could handle.

The car with the three old men stopped by Baker's pickup.

"It's stuck! It's stuck! You need to get it out!" Ingrid jumped up and down beside the goat, her hand over her mouth, her eyes wide.

"What's all the commotion about?" an older gentleman said as he climbed slowly out of his car.

Kenni had moved to look at the back of the goat. She really didn't know much about births, but she thought sometimes they were slow. But even if the goat was stuck, she didn't know what to do about it. Did she just grab a foot and pull?

"Never mind about that. What are you doing with Billy?" the man asked gruffly.

Kenni's head jerked around. That name sounded familiar. Who was Billy?

"Billy?" she asked, feeling like she hadn't made a rational statement in a really long time.

"That steer. He's got one of the little piglets on him. Did you steal it?"

She looked where he was pointing, and sure enough, over beside the barn there was a familiar-looking, large, shaggy steer, with horns that must be at least two feet long sticking out both sides of his head, and standing on top of his neck, with its little snout peeking up over the top of the steer's brown fur, was a miniature pig.

She recognized the steer as the one Baker had said was a matchmaking steer. The one she had been hiding behind when he'd said it. Not even twelve hours later, they were married.

She had to believe the rumors. Still.

"I promise you. I did not steal that steer or that pig." No matter how cute it was. "And I honestly don't think I can handle trying to steal anything right now, especially something that needs to be fed. I do not purposely try to make myself more crazy than I already am."

That probably wasn't the best answer she ever gave, but she didn't know what else to say.

"That pig's gonna need its mom. I don't think it's time to wean them yet. Have you heard?"

"I'm Kenni. I'm new here. I have no idea what you're talking about." She held her hand out, just because she'd always been told it was a polite thing to do when introducing herself, even though she felt a little bit like screaming as the goat and the calves baaed and bawled in harmony around her.

"Oh! You're Baker's wife. I heard about that. You must have heard the men get snatched up pretty fast around here, so you didn't waste any time when you came into town." The man guffawed like that was some kind of joke.

"Mr. Marshall! Mr. Blaze! Mr. Junior!" Darby called from the house. Then she looked at Kenni. "I'm so sorry to barge in like this. But my daughter has piano lessons in Rockerton in two hours, and I have to go home and take care of my chicks before I can take her, and we need to get this done quickly."

"It's okay. Make yourself at home."

She almost added "make the kids breakfast while you're at it," but she didn't. Maybe she should have. Perhaps if she'd been there for longer than one day, if she'd known Darby for more than five minutes, or if she'd ever delivered anything in her life before, she'd have felt more comfortable ordering people around. But as it was, it was obvious that Darby was on a time crunch, and the men were dawdling.

"Gotta make sure that someone takes care of that pig. She can't be away from her mom."

"I'm sure Billy will take care of it. Now, are you going to come in and film this Oreo cookie brownie cheesecake?" Darby asked, one hand on her hip.

She knew how to whip the men into shape, apparently, since they all started shuffling toward the door. Except for one. "I want to see this baby be born. I've never seen one before."

"There's gonna be a lot of blood and guts. Trust me, you're better off with the cheesecake," one of the other guys said over his shoulder.

"You have to get in here."

"Can't we film it here, in front of the birth?"

That made Kenni's stomach turn. The last thing, very last thing she wanted to see in a cooking video was a goat having a baby behind whoever was mixing the ingredients up, but the other two men seemed to think it was a wonderful idea, and one of them said, "Get out here, Darby. We'll set this stuff on the hood of my car and get a camera angle so we can have the goat having her baby in the background."

A gust of wind shook the big bushes that grew beside the driveway. They rattled and twisted and reminded Kenni that she was supposed to make sure the plastic somewhere was tied down before the storm.

She had been in the middle of not being able to handle her life when the men had pulled in, and she was going to text her husband.

"I think the goat is going to die!" Ingrid said, clutching Alice and burying her head in Alice's shoulder, wailing.

Kenni had her phone in her hand, ready to send a text to her husband, when it buzzed before she could unlock the screen.

It was a message from her husband.

The cows are out. Can you go over behind the barn and head them off. Just wave your arms and yell at them, and scare them back toward us so we can get them back in. Please.

Well, at least he said please. Politeness and manners were extremely important when a person's life was exploding in front of their face.

"Hey, honey, could you move to the side a little bit so we can get the goat's butt and the baby's nose in the background there? Go ahead and dump the cream cheese in the bowl, Darby, and put your head down a little so I can get you in the shot as well," one of the old men called from behind her, and Kenni moved to the side as she had been asked.

The calves bawled, the goat baaed, and the wind gusted even harder.

She looked around frantically, trying to figure out which way the cows were going to come and where she should go to head them off and if it was safe for the kids to go with her.

Her stomach growled, and she no sooner thought that she would have a lot of things to do before she was able to eat than Henry grabbed a hold of her shirt and tugged. "I'm hungry."

"Well, I'm hungry too. But I think we need to wait a little bit."

She didn't know what else to say, but that wasn't what Henry wanted to hear, and his face scrunched up.

"You think you could help me chase cows?"

Her husband wouldn't ask her to do anything that was dangerous, would he?

She honestly didn't know him well enough to be sure about that. She knew he would protect her. Defend her. And do his best to keep her safe. But that would be from human predators.

Would he ask her to put herself in front of a herd of cows to turn them, knowing that there would be danger involved?

"Yes! I want to do that!"

"All right. Let's do it together," she said, grabbing his hand and saying to Alice and Lucas, "Can you two stay here? I'm going to take Henry with me, because I need to do something with the cows."

She wasn't sure exactly what she was supposed to do. Wave her arms and look scary, apparently.

But as she and Henry took two running steps toward the barn, seven black cows ran around the corner, directly toward the house.

The cars were between the cows and the house, but that didn't seem to make any difference; they were charging at full speed and did not slow down as they swerved around the vehicles, knocking the ingredients off the hood as Darby grabbed Alice and Luna close to her and the old men scrambled onto the hood.

Kenni, already holding Henry's hand, grabbed Lucas, who held Theodora, and then took a hold of Ingrid's hand, and gathered the children in a bunch, hunching down in front of the pickup.

Surely the cows wouldn't make a sharp right after they came around the pickup?

"Are you getting this all on video? This is going to go viral for sure!" one of the old men said.

"I just hope they don't hurt my chicks," Darby said, and Kenni wasn't sure whether that was a prayer or whether it was just her thinking out loud. Maybe both.

She almost added her big concern to the rest of theirs. After hoping the children didn't get hurt, she just hoped they didn't chase the cat into the next county.

If there was going to be some kind of loss today, she prayed it was only pounds off her waist from not eating. Was it suppertime yet? Bedtime? Bedtime would be even better.

Somehow her only goal for the day had degenerated into hoping that she didn't let anything die.

Chapter 12

B aker hoped that Kenni had gotten his last text when he told her to never mind about chasing the cows.

They were going too fast, and she wasn't going to be able to stop them.

He didn't think the cows would run her over, and he was pretty sure that she would be smart enough to get out of the way.

Regardless, he urged his horse to go faster, when normally, if he were following runaway cows, he wouldn't be galloping behind them.

But Chester responded to his urging, galloping beside the barn and around the corner.

Baker couldn't help it; he pulled his horse to a stop and surveyed the scene before him.

To his left, just peeking out from behind the shed beside the barn, was Billy, the Highlander, from Sweet Water. Perched on top of Billy's neck, with its snout looking tiny between the large mass of horns, was a piglet. Probably one of Munchy's babies. Perhaps it was sleeping on Billy's back when Billy got up and wandered the four miles from Gideon's house to his.

Regardless, that was not the most unusual thing in his yard.

It looked like ingredients to make some kind of dessert were scattered around where the vehicles were parked, and he was pretty sure that Blaze, Marshall, and Junior looked a little abashed as they glanced over at him. Darby was the only one moving as she glanced at the kids—kids? —at her side before bounding in the house.

Elias had told him that Darby had been taking her chicks with her wherever she went, and Baker could only assume that she was running in to check on them.

Apparently she had lost a bunch, and after crying for an entire afternoon, she had determined that she would never lose another animal again.

Baker could have told her that if she was going to be a farmer, there were going to be more than chicks dying, but he understood her determination to make sure that her babies were okay.

Still, he couldn't quite wrap his eyes around the other thing that was going on. And that was...apparently a birth.

One baby kid lay on the ground, the mother licking at it, while two more little hooves stuck out from her rear end.

Gideon's kids, whom Baker had forgotten until just that moment were going to be let off at their house this morning, gathered around, in a semicircle, watching the baby and pointing and laughing.

The yard looked a little trampled, like his cows had gone through it, but they were nowhere in sight.

The bawl of his calves broke the silence, then the baa of the goat followed it.

He assumed that meant the calves hadn't been fed. They shouldn't be bawling unless something else had happened.

His eyes took another split second to sweep his front yard again, wondering if he'd missed anything.

On the third sweep around, he saw Rainbow, his cat.

No wonder he'd missed her the first two times. She had climbed into the bush that grew beside the house, and only her nose and ears peeked out from the top of it.

What was she doing outside?

He moved forward just a little bit, and his wife, standing up in front of his pickup, came into view.

It didn't look like she had combed her hair that morning, and she looked more ruffled than he'd ever seen her.

Frazzled. Maybe a little shell-shocked. Possibly the way he looked after he'd been rescued from the hostage situation where he'd been taken captive for six hours.

He recognized that look. He'd seen it on his friends, too.

"Whoa, boy," he said, patting Chester's neck as he swung a leg over the saddle, landing on the ground, and led his horse to the pickup.

"Kenni?" he said, carefully and gently.

The goat baaed, and Kenni took a look at the kids before she raised weary eyes to his.

"I said a lot of great things yesterday. Stuff about being able to handle things. I take them all back."

He grinned. He was pretty sure she was joking. "You're not going back on your wedding vows, are you?"

"I meant those. But I'm pretty sure I saw the 'for worse' part of for better or for worse this morning."

Just then a gust of wind blew, blowing her hair across her face and gusting so hard he had to lean into it to stay upright.

"I'm going to assume you didn't get the plastic secured."

That wasn't a question, but she shook her head no.

"I'm sorry," she said, and she sounded dejected. Like she was a failure.

"Looks like you've had a day that probably will never be repeated. I promise, most days are...not quite this bad."

"You warned me. Yesterday. You said about all the work. I thought... I thought I could handle it."

"You can. You are. You have."

"I haven't gotten anything done today. Nothing."

"Has anyone died?"

"Not yet. Please. Don't jinx anything more than it's already been jinxed."

"Relax. You've got a brand-new baby on the ground. She's already trying to get up and eat. And look, the second one just slipped out." He paused for just a moment. "Who brought the goat?"

"A man who talked slow and spit a lot."

"Gene." He laughed. "He said he was coming. What did he do, dump it off and leave?"

"The feet were sticking out, he knew it, and he left anyway. Laughing the whole way."

"He's a good neighbor. I like him."

"Good," Kenni said. "I've been thinking about taking up spitting as a habit. It's nice to know you're gonna be okay with it."

"Hold up here. I didn't say anything about—"

"There's another one!" one of the kids called.

Kenni turned, and Baker put his arm around her. She leaned into him.

She'd had a lot of excitement, and he had to say he was very pleased at how she had handled it.

"I guess we are going to have a goat herd now. Interesting," he said.

"And that's how you roll with things around here?" she asked.

"That's how you roll with things. Are...are you gonna be okay if I go get my cows in? I'd really like to have them in before the storm."

"Sorry I let them go."

"I texted you and told you to stand back. You weren't going to be able to stop them as fast as they were going."

"Oh." She looked at her phone like she'd forgotten she was holding it in her hand. Turning it over, she saw his text. "All right. I guess I'll let you go ahead and handle the cows. Is it terrible that I feel like I'm six steps behind everyone else here today?"

"You're doing fine... Do you want me to stay here and help you?"

"Well, I don't have the kids fed, I don't have the calves fed, I lost your cat, and I'm not sure what to do about the goats." Her head turned toward the barn. "I couldn't have gotten less done, and do I need to do anything with the steer?"

"I suppose I can put them in the barnyard until after the storm. Not because Billy can't handle it, but because the piglet might get cold."

"Would it be hungry?"

"Probably."

"Seems like everything on the farm is hungry today."

"That's pretty much the way it goes every day. We feed a lot of stuff. Every day. Including ourselves."

She smiled. "Did you get anything to eat?"

"No. I didn't even get coffee this morning."

He didn't bother to tell her why he rushed out of the house, that he got a text from the neighbor that his fence was down, and his cows were out.

"Is this how every day is?"

"Not every day. But there's almost always something going on. Some kind of issue, some kind of problem. You just do a lot of fixing things, feeding things, problem-solving. That's life on the farm."

"All right." She smiled. "At least I know what I'm getting into now. Yesterday, I was kind of naïve."

"I think there are a few more things we'll probably both need to learn. I've never had a day quite like this."

"She had the third one!" the kids yelled from behind them, and they both smiled, looking at each other, then back at the kids.

"I... I thought maybe I'd talk to you about this later, but I decided today that I'd like to have children."

He stilled. Then he laughed. "So she doesn't get scared off, she decides that the best way to meet the problems is to go charging headlong into them?"

"I never claimed to be smart."

Chapter 13

Just seeing Baker for a few minutes rejuvenated her spirit.

As he rode away, she took a deep breath and turned around at the chaos in front of her.

A gust of wind, stronger and more ominous, reminded her of the impending storm.

She had never been in North Dakota during a thunderstorm, but considering how wide open the spaces were, she could only imagine that it could end up being pretty fierce.

Just then, lightning sliced through the sky, and a few seconds later, the thunder boomed.

She needed to get the kids rounded up, but first, the old gentlemen who were there, along with Darby, were chasing after their things.

It was the cows' fault, but she ran over, grabbing a box of cream cheese as it blew off the top of the car hood.

"I'm sorry about the garbage through your yard," Darby said as she ran after a grocery bag.

"It's okay. It's not like you can help it," Kenni said as she ended up on her hands and knees, picking things up.

Glancing over her shoulder, she saw the old men with two kids, grinning and smiling while they looked at the goats and still taking videos.

"I have to admit, the kids are a cute addition to the videos," Darby said, also on her hands and knees as she crawled up beside Kenni.

"I guess if you're trying to go viral, that might work."

"Everyone likes to see a catastrophe. We couldn't have planned this better if we tried. This is much better than actually having the recipe turn out."

"If you say so."

"I could be wrong, but I bet it will be." She glanced at her watch before she looked back up at Kenni. "I left all the ingredients to make a second one in the kitchen. That was payment for letting us use your... We planned on the kitchen, but it ended up being your yard."

"Oh. Thanks. You really didn't have to." She didn't think she was speaking out of turn. After all, she had married Baker yesterday, and the house was...theirs?

She wasn't sure.

"I need to grab my chicks and head in to pick up my daughter for her lessons. Jonah rigged up a way for me to use the heat light in my car."

"I hope they make it okay."

"Me too. There's nothing worse than coming home and seeing that you trusted something to work, but it didn't, and you killed an entire batch of chicks." Darby shuddered, closing her eyes, almost as though the thought hurt.

"I can't even imagine," Kenni said, sincere.

"Let me help you get those goats into a pen, so they'll be out of the rain before it hits, before I leave."

"Oh, I would appreciate that." Kenni tried not to sound overwhelmed, but she definitely felt overwhelming gratitude.

"What a day and what an initiation to farm life. It isn't always this bad. I promise," Darby said as she grabbed a hold of two of the kids and indicated the third one with her head. "Can you grab that one? I think the mama will follow us if we're carrying her babies."

"All right, I got it," Kenni said, looking back at the mama who followed her kids eagerly. "I think they were eating, weren't they?"

"Yeah. That's definitely something you want to watch. But it looked to me like all three of them were trying to find food."

"All right. Make sure they eat," Kenni murmured, almost to herself.

Darby helped her find a spot in the barn. Lucas and Henry, who had followed them in, gave them a hand spreading some hay out for a cozy bed. The mama goat started to eat it.

"If you want me to, I can watch the kids while you feed the calves. I assume that's why they're bawling?" Darby said as they came out of the barn, looking at her phone, then squinting at the black clouds in the distance. They seemed to be rolling closer by the second.

"Please. If they want to help me, they can, I just... I only did it last night, and that was mostly watching Baker as he showed me how."

"All right. I'll either help you, or watch the kids, or a combination of both," Darby said, and she was as good as her word, following Kenni as she went to the sink, got the bottles, and made them the way Baker had shown her.

As they walked out to the calves, Ingrid and Alice both begged to hold bottles.

Thankfully, the calves were still alive and very hungry. They took the bottles eagerly, and all Kenni had to do was stand back and watch.

It was easier than she thought and only took fifteen minutes, tops.

They were taking the dirty bottles back to the house to get rinsed off, with Darby talking about her chicks and the impending storm, when another car pulled down the drive.

"Oh no," Darby said, with enough emotion in her voice that Kenni stopped, staring at her friend.

"What?" she asked, looking at the sky. The lightning had gotten closer, the periods between the lightning and thunder getting shorter. But she thought they still had a few minutes before the storm hit.

"That's Miss April. And her niece. The reporter."

"Oh." Kenni's chest seized tightly, panic swelling her throat. She was going to be found out. There was no way she could hide the fact that she was completely inept and not look like a princess.

"All right. Here's what we're going to do. I assume that you're hiding from the paparazzi and don't want the rest of the world to know that you're here. I'll simply tell them that you and Baker are enjoying a honeymoon and would prefer to be left in peace."

"That sounds wonderful, except we have six kids, and a whole barnyard full of animals, as well as you, your chicks, and the old men who were making TikTok videos here! It hardly rings true. Especially since I don't even know where Baker is!"

Darby had stopped, and she was tapping her upper lip. "I don't know about Miss April, but I've always liked Eliza. She...has been around a few times in Sweet Water and seems like a really great person. I... If she weren't part of the paparazzi, I would trust her."

"All right. I'll keep that in mind. But I know you don't have time to spare. You need to get your chicks home. And I know you want to carry them out before the rain starts. Let me help you. I'll get the light. And thanks so much for helping with the calves."

"I can help!" Alice chirped up from beside her.

"Perfect. When we walk out, you can open the door for us."

"I want to help too!" Ingrid said.

"You can open the car door, okay?" Kenni said. And Darby gave her a smile. Like she hadn't expected her to try to include the children in what they were doing.

She supposed that wasn't a very princess thing to do, but she hadn't ever been a typical princess.

They went into the house, rinsed the bottles out, and met Miss April and Eliza on their way out.

Darby gave her a look, one that held pity and compassion and also inquiry. Kenni was sure that if she changed her mind or wanted reinforcements, Darby would stop what she was doing with her chicks and help her.

But she couldn't impose that way. Darby had her own life and needed to pick up her daughter. Kenni was going to make it out here. This was her first test, or maybe her second or third, she'd have to count up later, when she actually had time to catch her breath, and she was going to pass it.

The old fellows waved as they gathered around, climbing back in their car. They left right on the heels of Darby.

"Let's go in the house," she said to the children as they ran around her.

Then, she faced her guests as they came up the walk. "Hi. I recognize you both from yesterday." She squinted at the sky. "Let's head in the house. I understand we have all the ingredients to make an Oreo cookie brownie cheesecake, and it looks like it's going to rain here any second anyway."

"That sounds wonderful," Miss April said, putting her purse over her head as the first big drops splattered to the ground.

"Oh my goodness, those are the biggest raindrops I've ever seen!" Eliza said, laughing as she skipped up the walk beside Henry and Ingrid. They had taken one look up into her sparkling brown eyes and had stuck like glue to either side of her.

That made Kenni raise her eyebrows. She'd always heard that dogs and children could tell a lot about people, and after what Darby had said, Kenni thought that maybe Eliza wasn't as much trouble as what she thought she was.

"Oh!" She looked around frantically. "I forgot about the cat!"

"I'll get her!" Ingrid said, grabbing a hold of Eliza's hand and pulling her over to the spot by the porch where the cat had disappeared three...or was it four times already that day?

Kenni figured it was probably pretty sad that she couldn't even keep track of what all had been happening, but the day had been so crazy.

She had to hand it to Eliza. The woman got down on her hands and knees, then lay down on her belly, looking in the hole with Ingrid, as Ingrid called for the kitty.

To Kenni's surprise, the cat came out, none too soon, as they were able to get a hold of it and run into the house just before the deluge let loose.

"Love the way the rain sounds on the roof!" Eliza said, laughing as she stood right inside the door, looking down at herself and brushing at the dirt on her shirt. "I hate to get this all over the house."

"Don't worry about it. There's been so much going on here today, people in and out, that I'm sure I'll be sweeping and scrubbing after everyone leaves," Kenni said, laughing along with her and shaking out her own hair.

She'd be sweeping and scrubbing, after she figured out where the broom and mop were. After she figured out if they even had one. She left that part out.

"It doesn't look too bad in here. But since we passed two cars going out the driveway, and I know about the lost cat, I assume things have been pretty crazy."

"Oh, that's not even the half of it," Kenni said, and then she launched into an explanation of how her day went as she stood at the sink washing her hands and helping the kids get theirs washed as well.

They might as well make the Oreo cookie brownie cheesecake, since she didn't have anything else ready for breakfast. Or lunch. Definitely it was lunchtime.

"Is this what you were going to make?" Alice asked, pointing to the recipe that Darby had left on the counter.

All the ingredients were sitting beside it.

"I think so," Kenni said, looking the ingredients over, so thankful that Darby had been so kind and thoughtful.

"Lucas and I can make this if you want us to," Alice said eagerly, obviously hoping that Kenni would give permission.

Her first instinct was to say no. After all, she had no idea whether Alice's mother would actually let her make something like that or not.

But then again, if she had six kids, she'd need them to be doing something, because there was no way she could take care of six kids all day long all the time without them helping.

So, she clamped her lips around her "no," smiled, and said, "Sure. It'd be great if you guys could do that."

It wouldn't be a healthy lunch, but it would be food. Which was more than what she had right then, especially considering that Miss Alice and Miss Eliza were looking at her like they expected to sit down and have a nice chat.

"Would you ladies like some tea?" she asked, indicating the kitchen table with a nod of her head.

"I'd love some. I got a little more wet than I was expecting to get today when I got up," Miss April said, carefully trying to brush the water out of her hair.

"All right. I'll get some water on."

"Can we look at these?" Henry asked, pointing at the magazines the men had left on the corner of the kitchen table.

"You sure can. Just be careful not to tear them, because they're not mine." She had no idea what they were, but they looked like beef and tractor magazines. They might not keep the kids entertained, but she was willing to bet they would keep a grown man entertained for a while.

Henry and Ingrid grabbed the magazines, their eyes big, as they whispered to each other, then ducked underneath the table.

If that's all it took to keep them occupied, maybe watching them wasn't going to be so hard.

Lucas and Alice talked together as they opened the brownie mix and asked her for a bowl.

"I'll have to look, because..." She glanced over at Eliza. Then she just went ahead and said, "Because I don't know where anything is in here."

She started opening cupboards and closing them. The kids saw what she was doing and began to imitate her. Soon, they found a bowl that would work as a mixing bowl.

They didn't ask her for anything else, but when they came to something they didn't have, they just started doing exactly what she had done, rooting around until they found something that would work.

"You had an exciting morning," Eliza said, smiling as Kenni put cups and saucers in front of her guests.

"It certainly was. I guess that's life on a farm. Although, not every day is like this." She repeated what she'd been told, praying it was true.

"I'm sure it's not. A person couldn't stand it if it was," Eliza said, laughing. Then, her eyes grew serious as Kenni turned from the table and started opening the cupboards, looking for tea. She supposed she should have made sure she had tea before she offered it to her guests. Considering that men lived in the house, the chances were high that they had nothing but coffee.

She had seen the coffee maker and probably should have offered that to her guests.

Still, the old cupboards, with chipped white paint, were a little bit more shaggy than what a person might think of as country décor, but they gave the kitchen a homey, lived-in look.

She liked the way the white kept things bright, as well.

Chapter 14

In the fourth cupboard Kenni opened, she found a small package of green tea.

"Does green tea work?"

"That's fine for me," Eliza said immediately.

"I'll drink it as well, although I would like to have honey in mine if possible," Miss April said.

Kenni had seen honey two cupboards back, so she went and grabbed the Mason jar that held a homemade label and was half-full of honey.

She smiled, loving the fact that they had gotten their honey from their neighbor.

How quaint.

Definitely not something she would do in the palace.

But she had had a life before the palace. She wasn't going to forget that.

Finally, she filled their teacups with hot water and set the kettle back on the stove before settling herself into a chair facing the two ladies.

Maybe the gig was up. Maybe the paparazzi was going to come and storm the house, and she would owe Baker a huge apology. Maybe it would be the first time in her life she ever apologized to someone for not lying, but she wasn't going to be able to lie to these ladies.

"I just wanted to say right away that you probably saw me with the paparazzi yesterday. The ones who were looking for Princess

Kennedy." Eliza smiled. Although her face was friendly, her eyes were shrewd. "I recognized you right away, but I didn't say anything, because I'm not actually here looking for Princess Kennedy."

"You're not?" Kenni said, her mouth falling open, her words breathed out as an afterthought. Here she was, scared to death she was going to be found out, but Eliza wasn't looking for her.

Could she trust Eliza?

"No. I've heard that there is a recluse, someone who was disfigured in a terrible fire ten years ago, who lives around town. Every time I visit Aunt April, I've looked for him. She's caught glimpses of him in town, and there has been word, rumors, that I've picked up on, but I've never actually figured out where he lives. No one seems to know."

"Interesting. I haven't heard a word of that."

"Most people around haven't. He wants his privacy, and as much as small towns love to share information about our members, if someone comes here, looking to keep their past secret, we have a tendency to circle the wagons and protect them." Miss April's smile was friendly, and it made Kenni feel like she and Eliza really would keep her secret. "For example. Yesterday, the paparazzi were looking for Princess Kennedy Weaver-Payne. They left without getting any information about her at all. None." Miss April looked smug.

"But if you wouldn't mind answering one question for me?" Miss April said before Kenni could feel too good about the fact that she was pretty sure they weren't going to tell on her.

"Sure."

"Princess Kennedy, did you really marry Baker last night? I mean, without even knowing him?" Miss April giggled like a schoolgirl about to get a good dish of gossip.

Kennedy laughed. Her gut told her to trust them. That they were being true. That they were just ladies like her and weren't trying to get a story to sell to the papers, but wanted to know news about their neighbors.

She could understand that.

"That was a little crazy, wasn't it?" She smiled and snorted a little, because she still couldn't believe she had done it.

"I think it's romantic," Eliza said, her eyes sparkling. Eliza seemed friendly and real. One of those people who were curious and inquisitive, but sweet and kind and honest as well.

It made Kenni feel like she had found a friend.

"We actually knew each other when we were younger," Kenni said, thinking her tea was almost cool enough to drink.

"You did? Were you together then?" Eliza said, her face showing interest, her tea forgotten.

"No. Although I did have a huge crush on him. He was my older brother's best friend. You know, that kind of thing. But he didn't even know I was alive."

"Oh, I wouldn't be so sure about that. I've heard rumors that Baker had a high school crush he could never get over. It very well could have been you," Miss April said, leveling her gaze at Kenni and probably not realizing the hope that surged through her as she heard those words.

Could Baker really have had a crush on her when she was younger?

"I hardly think so," she finally said. "I think Zeke, my brother, would have told me."

"But you ended up marrying a prince. That's like a fairy tale."

"I suppose on the surface, it's like a fairy tale. But in real life, it's a lot more complicated and a lot harder."

"How so?" Eliza was all ears.

"Well, I think they needed to do something to bring attention to the royalty in Corinth, because they were going bankrupt. They needed to get people interested and involved, in order to justify continuing to fund it. So, he found an American to marry. That's always sure to get the press involved."

"Of course."

"And I was just a small-town girl from the South. Hardly anything to get excited over, but that was part of the lore. I was a commoner, and the prince had 'fallen in love with me.'"

She put that in air quotes, because Isaac hadn't exactly fallen in love. He'd just worked the press, and rather brilliantly, if she had to say so herself.

"He didn't really love you?" Eliza asked. For the first time, her eyes looked sad.

"Can we put this in the oven ourselves?" Alice asked, indicating the pan of brownies they had made that was now sitting on the stove.

"Do you have everything ready already?" Kenni asked, standing up and seeing that they indeed had the brownie batter on the bottom, and it looked like Oreo cookies in the middle, and a white batter on top.

"We followed the recipe. And we used everything she had set out. Although we got an egg from the refrigerator. I hope that was okay."

"Of course. Whatever you needed in order to finish it. I'll tell you what, since I'm up, let me put it in for you. Are you setting a timer?"

"Can you set it on your phone? That's what Mom always does."

"I sure can. How long?"

Alice rattled off the time, and once Kenni had the brownies in the oven, she set her phone timer.

"Can we look at magazines with Ingrid and Henry under the table?" Lucas asked.

Kenni smiled and nodded, the eagerness in his gaze making her heart twist.

Who would have thought that looking at magazines would be so interesting to children?

But Alice and Lucas grinned like she'd given them a whole bag of candy and couldn't get under the table fast enough.

Maybe that was the draw. Doing it under the table.

Whatever it was, she shook her head a little as she sat back down.

"You guys definitely need children," Miss April said before she barely got settled.

"We... I don't think we talked about it. But I would like to have them eventually."

"You and the prince didn't have any? It kinda surprised me because I would have thought that they would have wanted an heir to the throne."

"Well, I'm sure you could read all about it in the tabloids, but we couldn't get pregnant. And he wasn't interested in going to the doctor to figure out why. He felt we had a lot of time. I really love children. It would have made life in the palace a lot less lonely."

"You were lonely? I couldn't tell from the way the press talked about it."

"Oh no. I could never have shown my loneliness to anyone outside of the palace. The press would have gone crazy over that. It would have brought negative attention to the king and queen, and I definitely didn't want that."

"That's very self-sacrificial of you. I can't believe you were able to stay for as long as you did if you were that miserable," Miss April said, taking a small sip of her tea, her gaze full of compassion.

"Being in the palace was all about doing my duty. I knew when I married Isaac that my life was going to be drastically different. I... I thought it was going to be worth it. I thought he loved me. It was kind of a fairy tale. But I knew it was a fairy tale that was going to involve work. Don't appearances that are beautiful beyond words usually involve a lot of work behind the scenes?"

Both Eliza and Miss April nodded their heads thoughtfully. Anything that was beautiful, weddings, even supermodels, or yards or gardens, they were beautiful because someone put a lot of work into them.

"I almost want to say that's sad, again, but... We do that all the time. We put a lot of work, sacrifice, into things to make them look beautiful. I guess we just don't think about that in the type of situation that you were in. That there is a lot of work to make that pomp and circumstance look effortless."

"Exactly. The same thing would be true for the president of the United States. His wife doesn't go outside looking anything less than perfect, and that's not an easy thing to do. There's a lot of work that goes on behind the scenes before she ever sets foot outside. Same with movies. So much time spent on makeup and costumes and getting the camera angles just right. Why would people think that the royal family would be any different?" Kenni folded her hands around her teacup, a little chilly despite the warmth of the kitchen. Maybe it was the subject matter, because she didn't really enjoy talking about it; most people seemed shocked when they were presented with the idea that, like everything else in the world, being a member of the royal family took work.

"People were so enamored with you. In my job as a reporter, people talked about it all the time. Everyone wanted to cover you."

"Yeah. That gets tiring too. Imagine someone dogging your every step, reporting on your every word. Speculating as to what you meant. What you actually meant. Making wild stabs at the motivations behind your actions. Most of the time, they were wrong, by the way."

"I can only imagine. People always want to believe the worst things about someone else, and the more the other person seems to be above them, in money or status, the more they want to believe the negative about them." Eliza pulled one lip back and used a finger to trace the handle of her teacup.

It was almost like she knew exactly what Kenni was talking about.

"I'm sorry. I don't mean to malign the people in your profession." And, by extension, her.

"No offense taken. I was agreeing with you. You are absolutely right."

"Why do you continue in your profession?" Miss April said, looking at her niece like she'd never seen her before.

"Because sometimes there are good things that come out of it. Sometimes you do uncover things that the rest of the world doesn't know. Although, people have a tendency to believe what they want to believe, and even when the truth comes out, they won't believe it because they don't want to."

Kenni nodded at that. That was so true. Sometimes reporters would report the truth, but it would be dismissed. The truth was boring. It was the lies and gossip that were interesting, the speculation that caused people to start talking about stories, which made them popular, which made the money.

"Especially in today's day and age where the more interaction a story gets, the more it rises to the top. I would venture to say that the more controversial and potentially untrue things a story has in it, the more people interact with it, and the more popular it becomes."

"I would agree with that completely. In fact, my colleagues and I sometimes talk about that. About the fact that you need to put some stuff like that in your story, or people will be bored and click past. They want the scandals. They want the speculation. They want the hints of an idea that not all is as it seems."

"Unless it's about ourselves," Kenni had to add, smiling.

"Exactly."

"I'm curious about this recluse. Why are you looking for him?"

Eliza hesitated. She bit her lip, continuing to run her finger over the handle of her teacup, staring at it as though it held the answers to all of life's questions.

"I was fifteen when the fire occurred. I... I was in the building. The man I'm looking for, a firefighter, was the one who rescued me. I had passed out. And I was the reason he got burned. I was burned as well. By the time I had recovered, he had been moved to a different facility, and I never heard about him again. Just bits and pieces here and there, and one persistent rumor that he is in Sweet Water."

"You want to thank him?"

"I guess. Or just... I don't know, yeah. Thank him for saving me. And apologize that I'm the reason that he didn't escape the fire unscathed. He had burns on his upper body where everyone can see, I guess. Mine are hidden on my lower body."

"I wondered. I didn't want to ask."

"Yeah. I actually had been looking toward a modeling career. I had won several competitions and had an invitation to go to New York City that summer. I never went. The scars on my legs are...pretty bad."

"I'm sorry." She heard a lot of times when people had burn scars that they also had trouble walking, but she hadn't noticed that with Eliza. She didn't want to ask. She felt like she was already probing into Eliza's privacy. Of course, she had shared more about palace life with Eliza and Miss April than she had with anyone else, ever.

Of course, now that she wasn't a part of the palace, she could talk about it. When she had been in the palace, she had had to weigh her words, even with people she considered her friends.

She could never have been as frank with friends in Corinth as she had been with these two ladies in North Dakota.

They chatted a bit more, and Kenni had to admit she was sad when the ladies said they had to go.

Chapter 15

"I'd love to see you again. Please come back," Kenni said as Miss April and Eliza stood at the door, looking at the world that had been freshly washed by the storm that Kenni had barely noticed, since she had good company and great conversation at her kitchen table through it all.

"I'd love to take you up on that. I've been thinking about settling down in North Dakota, here in Sweet Water, so I can be near my aunt. She is the last of my family, and... Probably because of the things we talked about, I've been thinking about hanging up my typewriter, so to speak, and doing something different with my life."

"You're welcome here anytime," Kenni said, impulsively stepping forward and giving Eliza a hug.

After a moment of Eliza freezing, probably from shock, she hugged her back.

"And you too, Miss April. I hear good things about you in the town."

"Oh my goodness, I can't imagine what you hear," Miss April said, stepping forward to wrap her arms around Kenni and return her hug.

The ladies left just as the buzzer on Kenni's phone went off.

She walked over to the oven as the kids scrambled out from underneath the table.

She grinned at their eagerness. "Stand back, and I'll take it out."

"The directions say it has to cool for two hours before we could have any." Alice spoke sadly.

"Two hours? I'm hungry now!" Kenni said, giving the kids an impish smile.

They didn't have to follow *all* the directions.

"You mean we can eat it right away?" Henry asked, stepping forward eagerly.

"I don't see why not. It's probably going to be runny, and it might not look as pretty as it would if we waited until it cooled, but it will taste the same."

"Yay!" Ingrid and Henry said together.

Kenni, looking at the time, couldn't believe that it was already two o'clock in the afternoon. It seemed like she'd done nothing but run from one catastrophe to the next all day, although talking to her neighbors hadn't been a catastrophe. It had been...a lot better than what she had been afraid of. Eliza hadn't been what she had thought she was going to be, and that had been a pleasant surprise.

She might have made a friend.

She had to admit she almost groaned when, after she finished dishing plates out for the kids and prayed with them, she looked out the window and saw another car coming down the drive.

More, Lord?

And she thought her days as a working royal had been hectic.

At least, when her handlers had scheduled her days, they had scheduled downtime for her. Today, she felt like she barely had time to breathe.

Squinting, she was sure she didn't know whose car it was. Not surprising, since she was new in town.

"That looks like Mr. Tadgh, and maybe Ellen in the front seat. Not Miss Ashley." Alice came over and stood beside her.

Just then, her phone buzzed with a text.

A part of her heart skipped a beat, hoping that it was Baker. She chided herself. He was busy, and he didn't have time to be sending lovey-dovey texts to her, even if they did just get married yesterday.

Sure enough, when she pulled her phone up, it was Gideon.

> **Things are more serious than we thought, and we're going to need to stay here all night. I've asked Ellen, the neighbor girl, if she would watch the kids. She can't drive yet, so her uncle will be bringing her over to pick up the kids and take them to her house. I figure you're probably ready to get rid of them by now. Thanks again for watching them.**

She laughed. The kids hadn't been any trouble at all. She looked at Alice, standing in the doorway.

"You are exactly right. That is Tadgh, and he is going to take you to their house, where Ellen is going to watch you."

"I'll get the other kids," Alice said, without question.

If she ever had kids of her own, she definitely wanted to talk to Piper to see what she had done to train them, because she wanted her kids to be just like them.

They hadn't had too many squabbles, and they had been careful while they were cooking not to make a huge mess, and they made sure to clean up when they were done.

> **Your kids were a joy. If you need help, I'll take them anytime.**

She wasn't entirely sure what she'd be doing with her days—that one had just happened without her deciding to do anything—and whether she could watch kids or not, but she hoped she'd be able to make time with her schedule to help out if they needed it.

That's what neighbors in small towns were for, wasn't it?

She was pretty sure it was.

By that time, the kids had finished their cheesecake, had the magazines stacked neatly where they had gotten them, and they opened the door, careful not to let the cat out.

They were actually successful, for the first time that day, in keeping the cat in. She allowed herself a triumphant smile as she followed the children down the walk.

A tall fellow with laughing green eyes held his hand out as she walked up. "I'm Tadgh. Gideon said he would be texting you."

"He did. The kids are excited for Ellen to watch them."

She saw a young girl, probably not even fifteen, and she was helping the children into the car, getting them buckled into car seats, and answering their eager questions.

She looked like she was used to working, with short fingernails, her hair in a no-nonsense ponytail, and wearing simple jeans and a T-shirt, along with cowgirl boots.

Her cheeks had two bright spots of red in them as she waved to Kenni, not interrupting the adults as they spoke.

"She loves her cows the best, but after cows, she enjoys kids." There was no doubt as to the affection on Tadgh's face as he spoke about his niece.

Kenni, curious about why Ellen was living with her uncle and not her parents, kept her mouth shut, nodding at Tadgh's comment but not asking any personal questions.

This didn't seem like the time to get the scoop.

"We really didn't have much of anything to eat this morning. It's been...a little crazy around here."

"We work on a farm too. I understand crazy. We'll make sure the kids get something healthy in their bellies."

"They're probably not going to be too hungry, because we all just had a piece of brownie cheesecake."

"I can't believe the kids are leaving if you still have any leftovers in there."

"That must be a testament as to how much they love Ellen."

"I think they love her cows. They know when they come to our house, Ellen will have them out, giving them rides and letting them pet them. She has a couple of babies she feeds with the bottle, and I'm sure she'll have the kids doing that as well."

"Well, Ingrid and Alice have some experience, because they fed my bottle babies this morning."

Her bottle babies. That was such an odd thing to say. She didn't really think of anything on the farm as hers. After all, this was her first day, but there she said that just as casual as could be.

Maybe adjusting to farm life, at least feeling like she was a part of things, wasn't going to be so hard. Actually, the busyness of the day, as they ran around from thing to thing, probably made her feel more involved than anything else could have.

If she had had an easy day where she sat staring at the wall not knowing what to do, it would have been much harder.

She smiled, since the Lord knew what He was doing.

"All right. I told Gideon I was available if he needed anything, and same to you. If you need help, or if Ellen needs a break, just let me know, okay?"

"I appreciate it," Tadgh said, walking back to the door of his vehicle and getting in.

Ellen had the kids all buckled, and she sat in the front seat waiting.

It was interesting to see children who were so eager to help and so well behaved. Was there something in the water around here?

In her experience, what she had from her royal duties, children were often unruly and caused more problems than anything else.

She tucked that thought away to think about later and walked slowly into the house, careful not to let the cat out, wondering what in the world else was going to happen that afternoon.

Chapter 16

Ellen felt the letter burning a hole in her pocket. She had wanted to read it as soon as she got it, but while she wasn't hiding anything from her uncle, he was sitting beside her in the car when he grabbed the mail and handed it to her.

They had gone and gotten the children, and she spent the rest of the day watching them at their house.

At bedtime, she'd gotten them all in the car, and Uncle Tadgh had driven them to their own house, saying that Gideon and Piper would probably be home, but it would most likely be late.

The kids had gone to bed without too much trouble, and now, Ellen sat at the kitchen table, the letter in front of her, with the unfamiliar scrawl she knew to be Travis's handwriting because of his name in the return address.

She didn't think she'd ever read anything he'd written, and she took a minute just to look at his handwriting, seeing how different it was than hers. It looked more impatient, confident, like he'd written the address quickly, not concerned about mistakes.

She had a tendency to take more time with her letters, forming them each perfectly, wanting to make them look pretty. She had been known to decorate envelopes with flowers and hearts and curlicues.

There was nothing at all like that on the envelope that she had on the table in front of her.

Eager anticipation made her fingers shake as she finally touched the letter gently, flipping it over and pulling up the edge, tearing along the top.

She supposed he could have texted her, or emailed her, or some other social media type of thing, but it felt more intimate to see his handwriting, to know he'd touched the paper, that he'd taken the time to put a stamp on it and take it to the mailbox.

She flattened it out on the table in front of her, noticing that there was writing on both sides. She smiled and then began reading.

Dear Ellen,

It seems a little odd to start my letter like that. Like, we don't call anyone "dear" anymore. But isn't that traditional?

It doesn't feel too bad. Hopefully, it doesn't cross the lines of our friendship. Because that's what I want. Friendship.

I feel like I need to start off with an apology. I asked you to wait for me. I shouldn't have. I... I can't expect you to do that. Especially since I don't even know what my life is going to look like by the time you're old enough to...well. Just old enough.

Mr. Hansen wants me to attend college. He signed me up for community classes which start in the fall. I never wanted to go to college. I just wanted to do something to earn money. But he told me that while I might not make a living with the things I learn in college, it'll broaden my horizons. I'm sure he's probably right about that. I know there's a lot of things I don't know.

But there are a lot of things that I do know. Friendship for one. Because you taught me that. You do know you're the only person who's ever really been a friend to me? I can include my parents in that statement as well, since you know I don't know my dad and my mom never really cared about me. That to me is what friendship is. Someone who cares. Someone who's there. Someone who doesn't give up on you just because you make a mistake or a hundred mistakes, like I have.

Anyway, I'm sure you don't want to read about all the things I think about when I lie in bed at night. That's just one of them. What makes a good friend. A friend like Ellen.

So, I'll try to keep you updated with the things I'm doing. Right now, I'm basically fetching coffee for a bunch of white-collar office dudes.

This fall, I'll keep fetching coffee, and I'll be taking classes, too.

Mr. Hansen told me to watch and learn. So I'm trying to do that. He said that I had potential to be able to not just work in his company but start my own.

It's funny, because all I ever wanted to do was be a farmer. But Mr. Hansen pointed out that farms are expensive, and in order for me to buy my own, I need to make money somewhere.

That made sense to me.

I hope it's okay, but when I think about owning my own farm, I think about having a bunch of Highlander cattle. I guess watching you and seeing how much you loved your cows made me feel like a farm just really isn't a farm unless there are some cows on it.

Anyway, that's a lot of years away. That's part of the reason why I couldn't ask you to wait for me.

After all, it could be twenty years until Mr. Hansen is done teaching me everything, and I put the things in practice, and I have a farm of my own.

That feels like forever, but it might not even be long enough.

I can't ask for time away, and I wouldn't want to come back home, unable to see you, because we're both thinking about the feelings that we have for each other, instead of just wanting us to be successful as friends. I hope that makes sense.

Anyway, when I come back, I'm going to look you up and going to talk to you. Just as a friend.

I mean it. So, I want to hear about you going to dances with boys, and dating like normal teenagers do, and all the other things that girls do. Of course, I won't have any advice for you, and I probably won't be able to make any intelligent comments, but I don't want you waiting

> *on me, thinking I'm waiting for you. Because I'm not. Anyway, I hope*
> *we can still be friends. Good friends. Actually, not to put any pressure*
> *on you, but you're my best friend.*
>
> *Take care, and be safe.*
>
> *Travis*

Ellen sat and looked at the letter, one tear rolling down her cheek.

Then she read it again. And then once more.

She didn't want to be just friends. Even though she knew he was right. She was only fourteen. She wasn't old enough to be anything other than a friend, especially with Travis. Her Uncle Tadgh had always said that she shouldn't pay too much attention to boys and definitely shouldn't have a boyfriend until she was ready to get married.

He had said that having a boyfriend was pointless. It just sucked up a lot of time and didn't really teach her anything. That it got in the way of learning the things that she needed to learn as a teenager.

She figured he was probably right, but she couldn't help feeling the way she felt about Travis.

Still, she knew that she was too little to do anything to act on those feelings, and that when Travis offered her friendship, she needed to take him up on that offer and ignore her feelings.

Still, it made her sad.

Regardless, after she thought about it for a little bit, she went over to the backpack that she had brought and pulled out a notebook.

Walking back to the table, she got a pen and sat down and started to write.

> *Dear Travis,*
>
> *I don't think that's too familiar. After all, "dear" is something that a mom would call her child, isn't it?*

> *And there's nothing wrong with that. Nothing romantic about it at all. So, if you don't mind, that's how I'll start my letters.*
>
> *I don't like what you said, that part about just being friends, but you're right. That's what I feel for you.*

Ellen sat and chewed the end of her pen. Was that true? It wasn't entirely true. She felt more now, and from the beginning of their relationship, she just...had more feelings for him. The friendship feelings were still there. The feeling that she could tell him anything, that she could trust him, that she wanted to take care of him, no matter what he did. Weren't those all friend feelings?

She didn't want to lie to him, and she almost ripped the paper up and started a different letter, but then, deciding that it was true, that she had friend feelings for him, along with a few more, she let it go.

> *I won a goat milking contest at school.*
>
> *I know, you probably don't remember the goat milking contest, it's new. They added it this year, just because they thought it would be fun on our field day.*
>
> *That was the day when everybody else had to go to school after you graduated.*
>
> *You left, so I thought you might not have heard about it. I didn't get a trophy or anything like that, in fact, I probably had people making fun of me more than anything, but I really liked it.*
>
> *After all, I know exactly how to milk a goat, and the person that I was up against didn't have a chance.*
>
> *Anyway, there were a lot of people taking pictures of me, laughing, but I guess I just like that kind of stuff. And it didn't bother me at all.*
>
> *I figured if you had been there, you would understand. You always seem to understand how much my cows mean to me. Uncle Tadgh does too.*
>
> *Anyway, I promise that I'll try to make my letters about more than just my cows. In fact, you might be hearing a lot about my dog.*

I got an Australian Cattle Dog, and I'm trying to teach her how to herd cows.

I figured that would be helpful, because even though all of my bottle babies come in when I call them, when Uncle Tadgh wants to gather up any of the other babies, he has to go through the field and get them.

We don't have horses, which would make it easier, but even if we did, neither one of us can rope anything. So, a cattle dog will make our job one hundred times easier.

If I can train her right.

I named her Chewy. I know, that's not a very creative name for a dog, and there must be a million Chewys in the world, but she is a blue heeler, and she likes to nip on my heels.

In fact, right now, both of my heels are covered in scabs from where she has bitten me.

I've been working on getting her to stop, but it's a trait that is bred into heelers, and I don't exactly want her to not do it, I just don't want her to do it to me.

Regardless, I've taken to wearing my boots around the house. Although, until my feet heal up, it's going to hurt.

Otherwise, there's really not too much new going on. I'm still bottle-feeding Uncle Tadgh's orphans, and he and Aunt Ashley are excited about the new baby that's coming.

I'm excited about it too, mostly.

I already talked to you about that though, so I won't say anything more. I guess... I guess I just love the thought that someday I'll have my own family. I want a husband who is never going to leave me. Someone who will stay true, never cheat. Doesn't that seem like something that happens in so many marriages? So many cheaters.

I don't want to be in a marriage if I'm not the most important person in my husband's life. What's the point in getting married if that's the case?

Anyway, I know I'm just fourteen, I'll probably change my mind a hundred times. But in the meantime, it's nice to know that I have a solid friendship I can depend on. I don't have to be your best friend, but I like it that I am. And I guess except for my cows, you're my best friend.

Most of the time, people don't understand me. I'm just weird. After all, normal people don't like to milk goats, and normal people don't spend so much time with their cows, perfectly happy to do nothing more than brush them and make them look pretty, and not care about the latest clothes or the popular music or anything that's the new, or the earliest, or whatever.

As long as my clothes fit, and they don't pinch me in any place that makes me uncomfortable, I don't care what they look like.

That in itself is weird.

So, I guess if you don't mind having a best friend who's weird in a lot of different ways, I accept. You can be my best friend too. Not like you weren't already, but I just made it official. I gotta warn you, once you're my best friend, you probably won't ever lose that status. I have a tendency to be loyal, even when it doesn't make sense.

I kind of hope I'll outgrow that tendency, but I'm guessing not. It's probably part of my makeup. Like Uncle Tadgh would say, it's just the way God made me.

All right, I rambled a bit, but I guess that's what friends do to friends, right? You read my ramblings and it makes sense to you, because you know them better than anybody. That's true too. Even better than Uncle Tadgh.

After all, I would never breathe a word to him or Aunt Ashley about my concerns about the baby.

Thanks for listening. You take care too, and I want to hear how college goes. You can tell me all about the girls that you date and the dances you go to, although I kinda feel like you want to spend most of your time working. Dances are just a waste of time, in my opinion. But you already know that.

All right, take care.

Ellen

Chapter 17

June put her head down on the table, tears dripping from her cheeks onto the shiny wood.

She hadn't told a soul about what she found out about her husband cheating.

Partly because she was embarrassed. After all, what kind of woman was she if her husband wouldn't stay true to her?

But also partly because she didn't exactly know for a sure fact that it was true. Of course, her friend's husband had seen Wayne with another woman. He'd told his wife, and his wife told her. She knew in her soul it was true, but it still could be gossip.

As much as she was sure in her heart that it was as true as she sat here, confronting her husband always meant angering him, making him yell at her, and on the off chance, the very off chance that it wasn't true, she didn't want to rock the boat in her marriage any more than what she had to.

So she kept the news to herself, trying to reconcile the idea that she had about her marriage with the reality of it.

Of course, she also had to realign her thoughts about the future with reality. She thought she'd be married forever. When she had said until death part them, she'd meant every word of that. She certainly had not thought for one second that she would ever consider giving up on her marriage.

She saw herself as being a married lady in her eighties and nineties, if God willed that she lived that long.

But now...now her children would have a broken home. She would be a divorcee. She had a life stretching out in front of her with no husband. She would have an end date on her marriage. An end date that she had chosen, not because death had separated them, but because she had walked out.

But she really hadn't determined that that was the best course of action. Maybe it would be better for her to stay? Her children would have a stable home to come to for holidays. Her grandkids would have a grandmother *and*grandfather. She would have support in her golden years. After all, if she left, she would be facing the most difficult years of her life alone. All because someone told her something that may or may not be true.

A car pulled into the drive, and she lifted her head, wiping the tears off her cheeks, and stood up, walking over and getting a tissue. She blew her nose and tried to pull herself together.

She had decided that today was the day she would confront...no, not confront. She didn't want a confrontation. She wanted just to know whether or not what she had heard was true.

Taking a deep breath, she tried to compose herself as she waited for the door to open.

She reminded herself to stay calm. She didn't want to fight; she just wanted the truth.

Getting it was a completely different story. Her husband was not exactly known as a man of his word, honest, with integrity.

The opposite, in fact.

"Hello, Wayne," she said as he walked in.

He looked up, surprise in his eyes. She didn't usually greet him at the door. Hadn't for a long time. He was never in a good mood when he came home from work, and she had gotten tired of being given three or four grunts and an irritated, "Just leave me alone."

Maybe she should have confronted him at a different time.

Not *confronted.*

"June," he said brusquely. Then his brows crinkled. "Is there something wrong?"

She gripped the counter and lifted her chin. "I heard something a couple of months ago, and I've been thinking about it. I wanted to ask you about it."

"Quit beating around the bush and just ask then," he said, toeing off his work boots after loosening the strings.

"Did you cheat on me?"

His head was down. She couldn't read his eyes. He finished toeing off his other boot, then straightened, looked her in the eye, and lifted his brows, almost as though he were challenging her.

"I've never cheated on you. Ever. I don't know where you heard that, but it's a crock of crap."

He almost sneered the words, like there was some kind of problem with her for even asking him. For ever doubting his integrity, dubious as she knew it to be.

He hadn't asked for any specifics and didn't ask what she knew or where she heard it.

"I heard that you did from a reliable source. This person wouldn't lie to me."

"You can leave if you want to, but it's not true. I've never cheated." He narrowed his eyes at her. "Did you make supper?"

"It's in the oven. It'll be ready at the regular time."

"I'm going outside to work on my truck until then. See if you can get your head on straight until I come back in and quit believing people's lies."

He spit that out before he walked over to the back door, put his sneakers on, and stomped out without another word.

Maybe she should have said something. Stopped him. Tried to talk to him about what he had done, but she didn't know what to say.

How did she discuss that with him when he wouldn't admit that he'd done it? That would only start an argument. One she couldn't win.

He didn't leave an opening for her to tell him what her friend had said. Did she force her words in?

Feeling the tears prick her eyes again, she walked slowly to the kitchen chair where she had been sitting earlier and sank into it, putting her hands on the table and laying her forehead on top of them.

Should she believe him? When he had lied to her so much before?

But he sounded so believable. So confident. Like the idea of her thinking that he cheated was ludicrous, not even worth his time. He didn't even stop to talk about it. Like he didn't give it any time and neither should she.

Maybe she was wrong. Maybe he hadn't cheated.

But she remembered the one time she had seen a message come in on his phone. It said, "Hey there, sexy."

His phone had been sitting on the counter. That was back before she had a cell phone, and before she was able to open his phone and figure out how to look to see if there were more messages, she was only able to see that there was a second one, a picture, before he'd stormed into the kitchen asking what she was doing on his phone.

At the time, maybe she'd been a little braver than what she was now, because she held the phone up and said, "Who is this woman?"

He mumbled some excuse about it being someone he worked with.

He hadn't apologized, but he had sworn up and down that that was the first time she ever texted him.

Of course, June asked to see his phone so that she could prove it for herself.

He refused.

In fact, when she stood in front of him, insisting that she wanted to see it, he had shoved her out of the way.

She hadn't gotten hurt, she'd just fallen into the wall, but he had stormed out of the house.

Interestingly, two hours later, as she sat on the floor working to figure out how to get their phone records so she could see for herself whether or not he had texted that number, he had come back in, thrown his phone on the floor beside her, and told her that if she wanted to see it, she could.

She picked it up, and sure enough, when she checked, those were the only two messages on the phone.

But later that afternoon, when she'd been sitting at the table, finally getting the page from the phone company to load that would show her the messages from his phone, just the numbers, not the actual words, he stood at her elbow, insulting her, swearing at her, and telling her over and over again that she hadn't texted but twice. The two texts she saw.

Then, the page from the phone company had finished loading, showing hundreds of texts.

He claimed the two texts she saw were the only two, had sworn they were, had insulted her for not believing him, and she'd been devastated as she sat staring at the evidence of his lies on the screen.

He'd been mad. He'd screamed and yelled that she'd not believed him and had gotten the records. Then, he hadn't apologized, but he admitted that he lied, that they had texted, but it had always been about work, and he'd never met her in person.

She had small children who needed her, no proof that he'd done anything but text—and what was the harm in that—and so she'd worked on forgiving him and tried to move on.

What else was she supposed to do?

He'd acted like it never happened, like he hadn't done anything wrong, and life went on.

That all came back to her, now that something similar had happened.

The cheating she'd learned about was ten years ago. Had he changed? Or was that just one time of many?

She wasn't sure what to say or what to do. Wasn't sure whether she should work on forgiving him and keeping her marriage together, or whether she should call it quits.

Lord? I made vows. I said for better or for worse.

She sighed. This was definitely "worse."

Isn't that enough? He broke the covenant? Can I leave?

She didn't even really feel like was she was losing a whole lot personally. He didn't act like a husband. He didn't seem to care about her at all. He hadn't supported her through her cancer. He hadn't encouraged her or helped her. They never did anything together. They didn't have a relationship where he was even a friend. She didn't enjoy spending time with him. Was whatever it was they had—a marriage that she stayed in because she'd said she would—really something worth fighting for?

It wasn't a matter of whether or not it was worth fighting for.

It was a matter of whether or not she was going to do what she said she was going to do.

Wasn't that the question?

She had never felt this confused in her life before. If he had admitted to the affair, apologized, and asked for her to forgive him, and they could work on their relationship, it would be so much easier. She would gladly forgive, gladly work on it. Gladly try to move past it.

Except...he was known as being a liar. He would say whatever he needed to say in order to get what he wanted. What if he lied about that too? Lied about being sorry? Lied about wanting to start over? Lied about working on their relationship?

It didn't matter. He hadn't apologized, so she didn't have to wonder about those things.

Wanting a friend to talk to, her hand hovered over her phone, thinking about Miss Helen.

She would give her godly advice.

But maybe, maybe she just wasn't ready to talk about it yet. She wasn't ready to open up her heart and expose her soul to someone else.

This betrayal felt too fresh, too wrong, too hard.

Lord. I want to do what You want me to do, but I don't know what that is. Please show me.

God had never answered her in an audible voice before, and He didn't do it then, either.

Desperate, she grabbed her phone and pulled up her Bible app. It opened where she had left off reading in Deuteronomy.

Fear ye not, stand still, and see the salvation of the LORD, which He will shew to you to day...

"Lord? Stand still? I'm not supposed to do anything? You're going to handle it?"

The thought gave her excitement but also weariness. How long until He would handle it? After all, her husband had cheated more than a decade ago. She was just now finding out. Between then and now, God hadn't done anything. Even though God had known about the cheating.

Could she trust Him to take care of it?

Of course she could.

Then why hadn't He?

Maybe it just wasn't His time frame. Ten years to God wasn't any time at all.

It was a fifth of her life so far, though. She didn't want to waste time with a man who wasn't going to love her.

Wasn't that what life was about? Wasn't that what marriage was supposed to be about? Her being with someone who loved her?

Wasn't her marriage supposed to be a picture of Christ and the church? Wasn't she supposed to forgive as Jesus had forgiven?

Didn't Jesus forgive even when people didn't ask? Didn't he love them even when they were conspiring against him? Wasn't he ready, standing there waiting for people to ask for forgiveness?

He didn't turn his back on people just because they were doing terrible sins that would be hard to forgive.

Wasn't that what she was supposed to do with her husband? The kind of love she was supposed to give?

Lord? Do You expect me to be some kind of example?

The Lord was silent.

Regardless, it was obvious that she was to stand still. She didn't want to. She wanted to pack her bags and leave that second. To get away from the pain and heartache. If she never found someone who would love her the way she wanted to be loved, at least she wouldn't be with this man who didn't care about her at all. Who had disrespected her devotion and disregarded her love and took advantage of her submission and obedience, treating her like she didn't mean anything to him.

She had served him, consistently and compassionately, to the best of her ability.

Is this really what I get, Lord?

She couldn't help asking questions, even though she knew God knew best. She knew He did. There was no doubt in her mind that God's way was the best way. Just... She didn't want to stay. She didn't want to keep going through it. She wanted to walk out.

Swallowing, knowing that she had to endure dinner sitting across the table from a man who so obviously didn't care about her, she tried to focus her mind on the good.

There wasn't too much good in Wayne, so she thought about Bible verses that talked about joy and love and peace and compassion.

She thought about the kind of person she wanted to be. The kind of person that she wanted her kids to remember her as. Not a bitter old woman who got angry and stormed away, but a loving, kind, sweet woman who did what was right even when it was hard.

That was the legacy she wanted to leave. That was what she wanted to be and what she needed to work to become—like Jesus.

Still, in this instance, she suspected that it was possible that God might give her permission to leave. She wasn't entirely sure, but she did know that she wasn't going to move a foot to the right or to the left until she knew it for certain.

Chapter 18

"**H**ey, did you guys see this?" Mr. Blaze held his phone up.

Marshall looked over casually. He sat at a booth in the diner, with Blaze and Junior, along with Toni and Sorrell.

Merritt had been reading a book, and she had gone upstairs to their apartment over the diner.

Marshall figured that since she had a dad, she wasn't as interested in what they were doing anymore.

The thought made him smile. Elias had been the best thing that happened to those girls in a long time.

Definitely the best thing that happened to Miss Jane.

And they were so happy together. Expecting a little one in the fall.

"What's that?" Junior asked, squinting at Blaze's phone.

"It's a woman who commented on our video."

"There are thousands of comments on that video. Why are you singling one out?" Marshall asked, annoyed.

They should be thinking about the next video they were going to make, not crowing over the accomplishments of their last one. They needed to stay on it, or they would never get to where they wanted to be. Which was TikTok famous.

They needed another recipe.

Although, he had to admit, filming the disaster, the storm, the goats being born, the kids running around, all that had made for a great video.

"Maybe we should quit trying to actually make things and just try to survive disasters instead," he said thoughtfully.

"What?" Junior barked at him.

"This is our most popular video ever," he said, pointing at Blaze's phone, then putting his hands out. "People seem to like seeing disasters far more than they like to see success."

"I don't want to be the star of a disaster channel," Junior said, rolling his eyes. "You might be popular, but you can't feel good about yourself."

"Why not?" Toni spoke up. "If you're making people laugh, you're actually helping them. Laughing is good."

"You don't want to make them laugh at the expense of yourself."

"It's not really an expense. It's just doing fun things to get people to smile." Toni grinned, as though the idea appealed to her.

"What does the comment say?" Sorrell asked, looking at Blaze who still held his phone up.

"It says, 'You old coots are a riot!'"

"That's about what everybody else has been saying."

"True. But... There just seems to be something a little bit different about this one."

"Does she have a name?" Sorrell asked, leaning over the phone.

"It says Miss Agnes."

"Agnes. That's an old-fashioned name. She's probably our age," Marshall said, humoring his friend who seemed to be enamored with that one comment. One that didn't seem to be any different than any of the other four thousand comments they had on their video.

"That's what I was thinking. Although, she could be older," Blaze admitted, looking at his phone again.

"Ask her where she's from," Sorrell suggested.

"You probably want to find out how old she is first," Toni said.

"Where are you from and how old are you?" Blaze said slowly as he was typing.

He hit enter.

"You didn't actually send that, did you?" Marshall asked.

"Sure. Why wouldn't I?"

"Because. If she answers you, you'll know where she is and how old she is, but if she answers you, you know you don't want that kind of woman."

"How do you know what kind of woman I want?"

"How do you know if he even wants a woman?" Junior piped in.

"Of course he wants a woman. Wasn't that the whole point of the channel?" Toni said, rolling her eyes.

"No. The point of the channel was to make money," Marshall said, and he thought that sounded reasonable.

"No. The point of the channel was for us to catch chicks. After all, I don't want you to be old and alone the rest of your life."

"I'm going to be old for the rest of my life. That's a fact." Marshall didn't understand why people had such a problem accepting facts. If he couldn't change it, he just had to accept it.

"But you don't have to be alone."

"Being alone is better than being together with someone who makes your life miserable." He felt he had some experience in that, and the men would be wise to listen to him.

He looked at the girls, putting his finger out and shaking it at them. "You girls remember that."

"I don't know. Mom's pretty happy with her husband," Sorrell said, smiling.

He couldn't help but notice that Toni seemed a little sad. Like the idea that she might have been happy for her friend, but she still wanted a dad herself.

"I know that. But just because she tells me how old she is and where she lives doesn't make her a bad woman."

"You want a woman with a little bit more...reserve. You don't want somebody who just lays everything out there for anybody who wants to know. After all, if they do that now, they're going to do that after you're married. There won't be anything special between you and her. She'll be telling the world everything all the time, and it will be annoying."

"To you. Maybe I like that kind of woman. Maybe I want someone who's not afraid to talk to people and doesn't treat everything like it's state secrets."

"There's something to be said for state secrets. That's why every state has them," Marshall said, feeling like Blaze hadn't learned anything in his eighty-some years.

Thinking the idea of a woman who would just tell some random stranger how old she was and where she lived was appealing. Yuck.

"Hey! She answered me!" Blaze said, holding his phone up, then pulling it down and clicking. "She said…" His voice faded off. He narrowed his eyes at Marshall. "She said, 'I don't give that kind of information out to random strangers.'"

"Ha!" Marshall said, grinning. Now that was his kind of woman.

He lifted his head. Actually, *that was his kind of woman.*

He grabbed his phone, pulling TikTok up and opening the app.

"Whoa. You can't do that. This is my woman. You go find your own," Blaze said, slapping at Marshall's phone, although Marshall easily lifted it out of the way.

"You guys are acting like children. Stop grabbing each other's phones," Sorrell said, rolling her eyes at their antics.

Teenagers nowadays. They were far more mature than teenagers were when he was a kid. Of course, he hung out with boy teenagers. He supposed girl teenagers were different.

"This one is mine. She answered the way I said she should, not the way he wanted her to, so obviously, it's my girl."

"She's not either one of your 'girls.' She could live in Florida. And then what are you going to do?" Toni said, finishing off the last of her milkshake.

It was summer, and her mom was a little bit more lax about her curfew, as well as her eating habits.

"Maybe I'd like to move to Florida. The winters would be nicer anyway."

"The summers will melt your dentures. They're miserable," Junior said, shivering, like summer in Florida was the worst thing he could envision.

"Summer in Florida couldn't be any worse than winter in North Dakota."

"No. It's not," Junior said, straightening up and shrugging, like he wasn't going to fight about that. There weren't too many things that were worse than winter in North Dakota.

Marshall had almost gotten to the point where he no longer considered it a fun challenge and thought about it more like something he wanted to avoid.

He was getting soft in his old age.

Of course, winter would be a lot nicer if he had someone to snuggle up with while the snow was coming down outside and the wind was howling and the temperatures dropped and stayed below zero.

He wouldn't mind that at all.

But like he had told his friends, he didn't want a woman who was going to blab all over the place.

Stealthily, so they didn't notice, he looked down at his phone, seeing Miss Agnes's profile pic and the comments she had made.

Agnes. That was a woman's name. Not some perky-cheeked little girl. A woman who had had a full life and would want to settle down in her recliner, snuggled under her blanket, content to relax and enjoy their golden years together.

He wouldn't mind learning more about this Miss Agnes.

Inconspicuously, while the conversation went on around him, he clicked on her picture, going to her profile.

TikTok would tell her that he had viewed her profile, but he was okay with that. Maybe that would make her curious about him, and she would check him out.

In the meantime, he looked at her videos, not noticing until later that night that there was one in particular of interest.

Not because of what happened in the video, it was just a bunch of ladies sitting in a car, getting stopped by the police, but because in the background, after he paused the video and went backward a few seconds, he saw the name of the town that they were in on a mileage sign along the highway.

Good Grief, Idaho.

It might be time for him to make a little road trip.

Chapter 19

"**I** need to get back to Kenni. She's been alone at the house all day."

"She'll be fine," Zeke said dismissively, throwing another sack of grain on the truck.

Baker paused, looking at the brother of his wife.

He never thought in a million years that Zeke would be his brother-in-law. That Kenni, the little girl who had hung around them, who had turned into a beautiful teenager that he crushed on, shared his first kiss with, would be his wife.

"I can't just leave her alone, especially when things are as crazy as they were today."

"You're getting all caught up in the fact that she was a princess. You forget that she's just Kenni. She can handle herself on the farm."

"It's not a matter of her not being able to handle herself." He threw the next bag down on top of the last one. "It's more along the lines of the fact that I'm her husband now, and I shouldn't just let her try to deal with everything by herself. I should be helping her."

"Seems to me the wife is supposed to be a helpmeet. She should be helping you." Miller smirked, throwing a hay bale over on the side of the truck.

"She is. That's the problem. She didn't sign up to have her days turned upside down by all of the things that happen on our ranch. She wants to have a life too."

"She's hiding. You're helping. She should be grateful." Zeke's words were thrown over his shoulder, short and to the point.

Of course, Kenni was his sister, he loved her, would protect her with everything he had, but he also viewed her as a sibling. Not as a love interest.

"Guys. You can't have a good marriage if you just neglect your wife and expect her to be happy while you're off doing whatever it is you're doing."

"You don't have a real marriage, man. Did you forget it?" Zeke asked, finally stopping and looking at him.

"We said until death do us part. Both of us meant it. We're going to try to have a real marriage." He didn't feel like he needed to explain that to his friends.

They all believed the way he did. Surely it wasn't a shock to them that when he made a promise, he planned to keep it?

"If nothing happens between you two, you can just get the marriage annulled. Isn't that a thing?" Miller asked, leaning his forearms on the side of the truck, his words conversational, not angry.

"I don't know. It doesn't matter, because that's not what I have planned."

"Sorry, man. But you guys went to separate rooms last night. It's pretty obvious the marriage can be annulled whenever you want it to be." Miller shrugged his shoulders, and while his words still didn't contain anger, they were confident, like he had Baker's number and wasn't going to be hoodwinked by whatever Baker was trying to pull over on him.

"I haven't seen her in years. You don't just...move into someone's bedroom after you meet one day."

"You don't marry them after you meet for a day either. I asked you to watch out for her, not marry her," Zeke said, setting the last feed bag down.

"That just seemed like the best thing to do at the time."

"And you can undo it," Zeke said, shrugging a shoulder.

"Would you make a promise like that, a covenant to the Lord, and then break it?"

"Of course not. I wouldn't do it in the first place. Not unless I knew that I was standing beside the woman I wanted to spend the rest of my life with."

"Maybe I did."

"Really? You've never talked about her, never said anything about her, and then all of a sudden yesterday you were madly in love with her?"

"You're my best friend. We work together. I'm not going to tell you I like your sister."

Zeke paused, his mouth hanging open, looking at Baker like he was seeing him for the first time. "Did you?"

"Shouldn't the question be in the present tense?"

"So you're going to turn into an English teacher in front of me?" Zeke said, rolling his eyes, but there was no rancor in his words.

"I just want to make sure we're clear. I do like her. I think she likes me, although I think she'd like me a lot better if I were at the house right now helping her, instead of here."

"You can't just stop doing all the stuff that you normally do, to sit around and hold your wife's hand. Even if I get married, I'm not going to do that."

"No, but I need to make sure that she's taken care of. That she doesn't have too much going on. That she's not overwhelmed. Especially on her first day."

"Her first day as your wife?" Miller asked, seeming to find that statement hilarious.

"Yeah. Our wedding wasn't exactly traditional, but that doesn't make it any less valid. She needs some time to adjust."

"Take all the time you need. We've already decided that you'd be the one to stay home. We need to head out now, although we'll be back late tonight. But you do what you need to do with her."

Zeke, for all of his big brother bluster, truly did care about his sister. "She's just had some really hard knocks. I... I don't want to encourage you to get close to her, if you aren't one hundred percent serious about it. I know we made you get married, that was to keep everyone from having to lie for you...but I guess I never thought about the lies you'd be telling each other." He blew out a breath and took a step away before turning back. "It feels like a mess. But if you really like her... I don't know where she stands. I hadn't talked to her."

"I'll make sure." He pushed back away from the pickup, lifting the end gate and slamming it shut. "We talked about it a little bit, but there really hasn't been a whole lot of time to get into a big discussion. I'm pretty sure that we're both on board with making this thing last."

"Don't force yourself into something she doesn't want. She just got out of one marriage that reeked. I know she doesn't want to be jumping into another one that isn't much better."

"Hey."

"Nothing on you, just... Just I think a girl wants a little more than a day to decide that she likes someone."

"They can take forever to make up their minds," Miller said with a roll of his eyes.

"Or they can do it pretty fast. Sometimes you just know. Isn't that what love at first sight is?" Baker didn't exactly believe in love at first sight. He wasn't sure that he believed in love at all. Not in the mushy-gushy, I've got all my feelings involved kind of love. More in the I've made a decision to stay with this person and treat them with kindness and respect, putting them above everyone else in my life...*that* was the kind of love that he believed in.

He thought that was pretty close to the Biblical definition of love. Of course, what did he know? He didn't exactly have any successful relationships under his belt. But a lot of people didn't.

A lot of times, marriage was their one shot at having a successful relationship. He didn't want to screw it up.

They talked for a few more minutes about things that Miller and Zeke were going to do, and Baker assured them that he would take care of the farm while they were gone.

Finally, his friends pulled out, and Baker had to admit he felt a bit of weight pull up off his chest. He didn't want to let his buddies down, didn't want to not do his share for their business, but he had been aching all day to get back to his wife. If they were going to have a shot at making their marriage work, he wasn't going to be able to just dump things on her and leave. And he was going to need to apologize for doing that today.

He couldn't wait to hurry back, but on his way, he happened to look over and see a cow had separated herself from the herd.

That usually meant something was up, and sure enough, there were two little black bodies lying on the grass around her.

Twins.

Well, it looked like he wasn't going to get to go straight to the house like he thought. He needed to make sure these little guys were doing okay.

Thinking he would send his wife a text, he reconsidered when he saw the mama cow painfully headbutt one of the little bodies, knocking it away from her. Unsteady on its feet as newborns usually were, it stumbled to the ground.

Baker needed to move fast, or that one wasn't going to make it.

Chapter 20

K enni held her phone to the side, reading the instructions as she unwrapped the rump roast she'd found in the freezer.

Thankfully, all of the meat in the freezer had been labeled. She had sent Baker a quick text asking if she was allowed to use the meat that was in the freezer in the basement.

He texted back saying that she should help herself.

She could just hear him laughing, even though there were no laughing emojis in his text.

The idea of her, Princess Kennedy Weaver-Payne, getting meat out of the freezer, thawing it, and trying to figure out what to do with it to make something for supper.

Regardless, she ignored the fact that she knew if Baker said anything, her brother was going to rib her about it when she saw him next.

She shrugged, accepting it was what brothers did, and focused on figuring out her recipe. Hopefully she would have something that was edible tonight for supper.

That was the plan anyway.

Not that she had a whole lot of time to work on it. And she was going to have to quit to feed her calves soon anyway.

She had no sooner thought of that than the door burst open, and her head jerked up to see Baker standing in the doorway.

There seemed to be blood or slime or something on his shirt and jeans, but he didn't make any mention of that.

He looked a little frazzled, and his words were short when he said, "Do you have a minute to help me?"

"Sure," she said, shoving her phone in her pocket and turning the oven off before she walked away from the stove.

He didn't hang around to explain to her what happened but ducked back out the door.

By now, she was used to sticking her foot up to keep the cat from running out, and she did so before she slipped out the door, closing it quickly behind her.

"Do you normally have problems with that cat trying to sneak out?"

"That's one of the things I should have warned you about and didn't think of," he said, walking quickly.

"Well, I figured it out. And I've developed a bit of a technique to keep it in."

"Stick your foot in front of it? Then slide out the door?"

"Yes. That's it exactly."

"I don't want you worried about it. It never goes far and always comes back in." He shrugged his shoulders but never slowed his stride as he headed toward the barn.

"What's up?" she asked, not exactly irritated by his brusque manner but figuring that she was probably headed in that direction. Why did he always have to act like everything he was doing was such an emergency?

"I'm sorry. I had all the plans in the world of coming back here, apologizing for not being here, and spending the rest of the day with you. But then I found a mama with twins, and she was beating one of them up. That's what they do when they only take one. This little guy was going to die. And he still might," he said as he opened the barn door just a little, to show her a tiny calf, bigger than the goat she had seen this morning, but still achingly small compared to the bottle babies that were inside the pen.

"Oh my goodness. He's so precious."

"Yeah. He's a fighter. But I need to get some colostrum in him. I was hoping you would help me hold him." His face was a mask of concentration, and his focus helped her to be calm.

"All right. You're going to tell me what to do?"

"Yeah. I need to make a bottle first. We can use some hay to try to wipe him off. It's not too cold out, but it will be better for him if he gets dry."

"I don't even have a blow dryer, or I could use that."

"That would be perfect. Maybe when you get one, we'll have it on standby."

She laughed, thinking that was definitely not something she ever thought she would use her hair dryer for, but not minding in the least, if it saved a life.

He disappeared for a bit, then came back less than five minutes later, with a full bottle of what looked to be ordinary milk to her.

"This is colostrum. Within the first twelve to twenty-four hours, you want to make sure that a newborn calf gets a little bit of it in his stomach."

"I've heard of that with babies."

"Exactly. It's just a little bit of a different kind of milk, with antibodies and things that give them a better start in life. It's not a guarantee that he's going to die if he doesn't get it, but there is a much, much higher chance."

"I see."

"I know this guy hasn't eaten yet, but he's not that old. So we have a good chance. The thing is, I had him over my horse the whole way back from the field, and he doesn't want to stand up."

"That sounds painful. I wouldn't want to stand up either."

"Well, if it meant life or death, I'm sure you'd find the strength to stand long enough to drink a quarter of a bottle."

"I'm sure you're right." She watched while he positioned the calf. "So we're not going to feed him the whole thing?"

"No. Not nearly. That would be too much. The package just makes a whole bottle."

"I see."

"If we can get a quarter in him, I'll be real happy. I wouldn't try to feed him more than a half, though. If he starts sucking on his own. Calves will overeat really easily. And this guy isn't that big."

"You said he was a twin?"

"Yeah."

"Did his sibling make it?" she asked as he straightened out the hind legs and indicated for her to help him balance so he didn't fall back down.

"That's the thing. A lot of times when moms have twins, they'll pick one and only want that one. That's what happened in this case. The other twin is doing just fine. He was eating when I carried this one off. But the mom was headbutting him, didn't want him to have anything to do with her or her other baby. If he makes it, he'll be another bottle baby."

"Of course he's going to make it. We're going to make sure of it." Her words were said with more force than necessary.

Baker turned to grin at her, a look she returned. "That's what I want to hear."

"That's what we're going to do," she said with determination.

She watched as he arranged the front shoulders to lean against him while he tilted the bottle up, sticking it into the calf's mouth.

"He's not sucking." He let out a frustrated sound. "So, what I'm going to do is put the bottle in the side of his mouth, deep enough that it will drip down his throat, and hopefully he will swallow."

"He doesn't need to suck in order to get it out?"

"I made the hole in this bottle bigger, just for this type of thing. It doesn't bother them when they're sucking, but it allows me to get milk out without any effort from the calf. As long as he swallows, he's got a chance of making it."

From her position at the rear end, where she was mostly supporting the back legs, she couldn't tell whether the calf was swallowing or not.

"He's doing it," Baker said, and she could hear the excitement in his voice.

It seemed to take forever, and her back hurt. She wanted to lean a forearm on something, or support herself in some way, because leaning over holding the calf up was making her back ache worse than she could remember it ever aching before.

Maybe she was getting too old for this.

Or maybe she just had to get used to it.

"He's almost there," Baker said after what felt like forever.

"He swallowed a quarter?" she asked, thinking he must have changed his mind and fed the calf a lot more for as much time as it was taking.

"Yeah. That's good."

"So you think he will make it?" She couldn't help but ask. He'd already said that the calf might make it if he swallowed, and he wouldn't have any better information to give to her, but she just wanted to make sure. She wanted the little guy to live so bad.

She supposed part of farming was having patience. Just taking it hour by hour, day by day.

"He's got a good chance. I'd say once he starts sucking, we're in good shape. But for now, he's got the most important thing, and that's a little bit of colostrum."

"That's fantastic. Are you going to put him out with the other ones?" She wanted to see him with company to have friends since he didn't have a mom.

"Not for now. He's still pretty little, and we'll be feeding him a little more often than we feed the other ones. If we can give him a quarter of a bottle four times a day, he'll be perked up in no time. Then we'll have him on a morning and evening schedule eventually."

He straightened, and so did she.

The calf walked a little on his own, taking one step, then kneeling down and flopping onto the hay.

"This is a good place for him to lie. He'll be nice and warm here, until I feed him again at—" He looked at his watch. "Four hours would be ten o'clock. I think I'd better do that."

"Do you need me to help you?"

He sighed and looked at her. "It would be a lot easier if you did. But... I told you, I need to apologize. In fact, I'm sorry. I didn't intend to marry you, then leave you alone at the house all day today."

"It was a pretty busy day. I understand you had things to do."

"Well, I did, but I hadn't meant for them to consume my entire day. Not after just getting married so that I didn't have any time for you."

"I am a big girl. I can take care of myself."

She said that a little defiantly. She didn't need to be babied. She didn't need him to come around just because he felt like he owed her or that she was an obligation.

His look turned to one of confusion. "I said something that made you mad?"

She gave a self-conscious grin and looked away. Figures he would notice. But why would she tell him? He couldn't get better if he didn't know what he had done wrong. And if he was interested in getting better...

"I was a little offended because you made it sound like I was an obligation. I don't want to be an obligation to you."

"You don't want me to help you? You want me to leave you at the house and not pay attention to you?"

"No. That's not it." She ran a hand over her hair, able to tell by touch that it was sticking up all over the place.

She tried to smooth it down while she thought about what she wanted to say.

"Kenni. If you tell me what it is, I'll try to do better."

"I'm sorry. I... I want you to be with me. But I want you to be with me because you want to. If you're just here because that's what husbands do..." She said that in an affected voice, like he was following rules that someone else made up. "Or because you don't want me to get mad, then it really doesn't really mean anything. You know?"

"So, it's not enough that I'm here. I have to be here for the right reasons?"

"Yes. Exactly. I know that sounds dumb, but...it's important to me. It's important to me that you don't resent the fact that you have to come spend time with me. Otherwise, it makes me feel like you don't really care, you're just doing it to check off the boxes. I don't want to be a box you have to check off. I want you to want to be with me, or don't bother."

He nodded, thinking, and she appreciated that he didn't argue with her or try to tell her how stupid her feelings were. She knew it didn't really make sense. Saying it wasn't enough for him to just do it, that he had to do it for the right reasons.

"I suppose it doesn't matter to you whether I cook for you because I want to, or because I feel like it's something I have to do."

"I understand a person would put more time and effort into it if it's something that they want to do. If they want to make someone happy, they're going to care. Do what the other person likes."

"Yeah. But if I just slap food down on the table, even if it's something you like, it's not going to feel very good to you, if I have a bad attitude the whole time we're eating, just because I'm doing it because I have to."

"I see. I guess I understand how it can affect your attitude. That's one thing. But you're saying I can't be nice and just be doing it because it's an obligation."

"Right." She sighed. "I know. That's a high standard. Is it too high?"

"I don't think so. Because I really want to be here. I wanted to be here all day. I feel guilty that I wasn't. And I'd really like to hear how things went. It looked a little crazy when I came through here with the cows, and I'm not sure things got better. I'm pretty sure it's been a day for the record books." There was a little bit of humor in his tone, and she laughed. "Come on. Have you fed the calves yet?"

"No. I was a little late feeding them this morning, I wasn't sure how much time had elapsed between feedings."

"What time was it?"

"It was probably ten or eleven o'clock when I fed them."

"It's six now. That's plenty of time. We can go make them a couple of bottles."

He opened the barn door and then stepped back so she could go through.

She appreciated that little courtesy, just that little bit of saying he was deferring to her.

She waited for him while he shut the double doors, then, to her surprise, he took her hand.

"You gonna tell me about Miss April?" He laughed. "That was her car, wasn't it? Tell me I was worrying for nothing?"

"No. It was her and her niece Eliza."

"The reporter?" His footsteps stumbled, and he looked over at her with concern in his eyes.

"The very same. But it's okay. I'm pretty sure anyway."

"You trusted them?" he asked, his voice skeptical, like he thought maybe that wasn't the smartest thing that she could have done.

"Yeah. She seemed like such a friendly and sweet person, and she also said that she really wasn't interested in me but wanted to find someone who was living around Sweet Water as a recluse."

"A burn victim?"

"You know him?"

"I might. But I'm not sure I would give his name to her, or his location. Or anything."

"I think she already knows his name. He...was someone that she knew. Actually, the way he got burned was saving her from the fire. I'm not sure if she necessarily wanted to thank him, or visit him, or what she wanted to do. But she was much more interested in him than me."

"Hmm. I thought the person that he saved had gotten burned. At least, somehow I'd heard that they were in the hospital for a while."

"She said the burns she had were down her legs. That they had ruined her modeling career. And I got the feeling that she was self-conscious about them. She probably doesn't wear shorts or even knee-length dresses at all."

"That's too bad."

She didn't press him anymore. Just in case Eliza truly wasn't what she seemed, she didn't want to have any more information to give to her than what she already had. If Eliza proved to be dependable and loyal, she would ask Baker more about the mysterious man who lived as a recluse near Sweet Water.

"So tell me more about your day," he said, and he seemed genuinely interested as he mixed up the bottles for the calves, and they walked back out, each of them taking a bottle and feeding the calves who drank hungrily. She couldn't help contrasting that to the little guy that they were trying to save in the barn as she told Baker all the things that had happened.

She actually was able to put a little bit of humor into some of the things, like the cat, and the ingredients going all over the place, and her shock when she saw Miss April with the reporter.

He laughed along with her, and she found the retelling of her day so much fun that it took a lot of the sting out of anything she was still thinking was hard or unbearable.

"The whole day, I wondered if this was as bad as it got. And if I would be able to handle it, then something else even worse happened, and I not only handled it but kept getting more. But telling it to you now, it sounds almost...fun."

He laughed. "I hope you liked it. That's probably not a normal day, but I bet you have more days like that than you would expect to see. Days where things just happen one on top of the other, and you just kinda have to roll with it."

"I'll take your word for it."

"You know, you didn't really have a choice about marrying me, not much of one anyway, but we do have a choice about what we do for a living. Today might not be the best day to judge by, but you know if you don't want to be a farmer, we'll find something else to do. I... I want to keep my vows, but I never told God that I would be a farmer for the rest of my life."

Chapter 21

Helen closed the oven door, then set the timer for forty-five minutes. Normally while she was waiting for the meals to cook—she was going to take this one to Kenni and Baker who just got married—she would pull down her quilting and work on that while she listened to an audio on YouTube.

But she had been trying to be more considerate of her husband. To do things that he would like to do and show him she was thinking about him.

It seemed to have been working a little bit. Where she wasn't exactly trying to get him to do what she wanted him to do, but more...to create an upward spiral where instead of them ignoring each other and thinking the worst of each other, they both tried to be more considerate, more kind and loving toward each other.

She felt like she was doing a lot more than he was, though.

But she couldn't expect everything she did to be met with a reciprocal action from him. She had to be kind to him just because it was right to be kind, not because she expected him to return her kindness in ways that made her feel good or loved and appreciated.

That wasn't what her marriage, her life, was supposed to be about.

Sometimes she had to give herself that lecture over and over again. Because she wanted her husband to be considerate. She wanted him to think of her. She wanted him to do the little things that made a difference.

Oh sure, he helped with the laundry, even did the dishes three or four nights a week. Sometimes he got the broom out and cleaned, and he always put his clothes in the hamper and brought his dirty dishes to the kitchen.

She knew men who didn't do any of that stuff.

She supposed she should just be happy that he was as good as what he was, but she wanted more.

She wanted a tender look. A soft touch. Someone who took the time to know her, who wanted to know her. Who just wanted to see her smile.

Just something for no reason, something that showed he cared. That she was more important to him than anyone or anything else.

She wanted him to sit and talk to her, not just about the car that he was working on, but about hopes and dreams and what they planned for the future. She wanted him to be curious about her and ask her questions. She wanted him to listen to her answers and remember them, and keep them in mind so that when the subject came up again, he was knowledgeable about her.

That he wasn't shocked that seeing Mexico was on her bucket list. Or that she wanted to spend a week in Hawaii, or that her secret dream all of her life was to go to Iceland.

He didn't know any of those things about her because, as many years as they'd been married, he'd never taken the time to learn them.

And she realized that she resented it. Resented that he wasn't curious, didn't want to know, didn't seem to care.

Maybe part of the reason she had trouble wanting to do kind things for him, beyond the fact that he didn't seem to reciprocate, was the fact that he didn't seem to care.

But that was partially her fault. She had cared at one time. Had learned all those things about him and had been careful to do them, to apply what she knew to how she treated him. But somewhere along the line, facing his neglect and the fact that nothing she did seemed to change anything, she stopped caring.

She couldn't change him; she could only change herself. She needed to be better. Better as in more considerate, more kind, more thoughtful. That's what love was. And she had pledged to love him. She was responsible for keeping her pledge.

So, she grabbed her jacket, sticking her arms in the sleeves, and walked out the door to the garage where he bent over the hood of his true love, his '68 Charger.

He looked up in surprise when the door closed behind her.

"Is something wrong?" he asked right away.

He was attentive, and his concern showed he truly did care. Just not about the things she cared about.

"I thought I'd come out here and sit with you for a little bit. I'm waiting for the meal I cooked for Kenni and Baker to get out of the oven. I'm gonna run it over to them while it's still hot."

"So you didn't want anything?" he asked, looking confused.

"No. I just thought I'd sit here and watch you."

"Watch me?" he asked, tilting his head, a little bemused.

"Yeah. Remember when we were dating? I used to sit in the garage and watch you work? You were so sexy with the grease up your arms and on your shirt. You had a pair of blue jeans that were my very favorite."

He grinned a little. "That's funny. I had no idea. I just knew I tried to find reasons to work on the opposite side of the car so your dad couldn't see when I grabbed you and kissed you."

She laughed. "My dad liked you. I don't think he cared that you grabbed me and kissed me."

"Sneaking around was more fun," he said lightly, a smile curving up his lips.

She was glad she had come out. They hadn't talked about that in years. She'd almost forgotten about it.

"It's that little bit of danger that gives things an edge."

"Or something that's forbidden. We always want the grass on the other side of the fence."

He set a wrench down on the edge of the car, then put his hand back down in the guts of the motor.

She supposed that was true. Maybe they'd just gotten complacent with each other. There was no excitement. She knew he wasn't going to cheat, and he knew she wasn't going to cheat, and they knew what they were going to have for breakfast, and they knew pretty much everything that was going to happen that day.

No surprises.

Unless she created one.

She thought about that for a minute. So he liked a little bit of danger, a little bit of the unknown. What if she did something like that? Instead of waiting for him to ask her what she wanted, before she told him that she wanted to go to Iceland, what if she just booked a trip?

Maybe Iceland was a bit much. But she could book a trip to Mexico.

"Tomorrow, I need you to go get your passport renewed."

"What?" He jerked up, his head barely missing the top of the hood.

"You heard me."

"No. I seriously didn't."

"You need to go get your passport renewed tomorrow."

She pulled out her phone. If she was going to do this, she needed to do it. She couldn't beat around the bush.

"Why's that?"

She had long since gone past the age where she would be considered sultry or appealing, but she batted her eyes at him anyway.

"I have plans for you." She lowered her voice and gave him her best imitation of a sultry sex symbol.

That made his brows go up. She managed not to smile. She couldn't imagine that anything she was doing actually looked appealing, but it definitely made interest spark in her husband's eyes. Interesting.

"Plans?" he said carefully as he set an oily piece of car motor on the edge of the car next to his wrench and then planted both hands on the sides and looked at her. His brows raised.

"That's right. I'm kidnapping you and taking you away with me."

His face fell just a little bit. "You're not taking me out of the country, are you? You know I don't like to leave home for any length of time."

"But this is going to be exciting," she said, although her heart dipped a little. Obviously, he wasn't going to be excited about a trip to Mexico.

She should have remembered that he hated taking trips. He much preferred to stay home. She knew that, but...maybe she thought that the excitement of the unknown would lure him away.

"If you want to go, that's fine. But you'll have to find someone else to go with you. I don't want to." His words were clipped as he looked back at the car, as though trying to figure out where he was.

He grabbed the wrench and shoved his hands deep in the guts of the motor again.

Helen felt like crying. So much for her coming out and sitting and enjoying company with her husband. Now her feelings were hurt, and she wanted to go inside and pout for a bit.

Not to make him pay attention to her, just until she was able to get her emotions under control.

She knew better than to beg him to go. Once he had said that he didn't want to, he wasn't going to. And there really wasn't anything she could do about it.

Maybe she just needed to give up that dream of going to Mexico. Cross that off her bucket list and put something like...taking a trip to the post office on it instead.

She sat for a few more minutes, while he continued to work in his car, but the happy spirit in her heart was gone. What was the point in trying to be kind? Why? It wasn't like she got anything in return.

There she went again. Thinking about what she got. She didn't believe the teachings of the world. She believed that God was right, but somehow the worldly teachings infiltrated her brain without her even wanting them to.

Life, even married life, wasn't about what she got out of it. Life was about laying up rewards in heaven. Being kind to people who weren't kind to her, even if it was her husband telling her he wasn't going to go on a trip, and her handling that with kindness and a gracious attitude, rather than hurt feelings and a pouting silence.

Maybe if she were to take a trip to Mexico, she would be gunned down by drug cartels or something like that, and this was just God's way of keeping her safe.

She hardly thought that a trip to Mexico would end with her death, but she had to face the fact that if she wanted to go, it was going to be without her husband.

She just didn't really have any interest in going with someone else. She didn't get married to someone else, she got married to her husband. She wanted to be with him. Wanted to do and experience things with him.

Thinking about it, she realized she had two choices. Be content with no trip to Mexico, or find someone else to go with her to Mexico and be content having a husband who was not a terrible person. He had a lot of great qualities. She should be appreciating the great qualities that he had, and not complaining or fussing about the qualities that he didn't.

Of course, it would be so much easier to be married if her husband was more interested in doing things with her and making sure they were both happy.

After all, how many car shows had she gone to even though she had zero interest in cars or car shows or wasting entire weekends sitting in some parking lot with the hood propped up, while people exclaimed over the beauty of each motor that they passed?

Hardly her idea of a good time.

But, again, life wasn't supposed to be about her idea of a good time. It was supposed to be about her giving, her being kind, her doing things for people who didn't return the kindness back to her.

If she believed the Bible was true. If she believed that doing that would lay up treasure in heaven, why wasn't she working harder to be happy right now? She should be thrilled when her husband told her no, and she had to take up her cross and follow Jesus, depending on Jesus to help her be kind and loving and sweet.

It was all good in theory, but in reality, she had to admit she wished her husband would just make it easy and be nice to her.

Lord?

There was no answer. Of course, life wasn't supposed to be easy.

God wanted her to rise to the challenge. To be different than the rest of the world. How could she be different than the rest of the world if everything in her life was easy?

People would just say she was a good Christian because she had never been challenged about anything.

Taking a fortifying breath, she put her hands carefully in her lap and tried to focus her mind on the good qualities of her husband.

The fact that he had been dependable all those years. That he had been a good husband and a good provider. A good father to their children. That he was kind and considerate about a lot of things that many men weren't.

And she knew if she needed him, truly needed him, he would do whatever it took to help her.

Settling her mind back down, focusing on the things about him that she loved and admired, helped a lot, and she managed to sit in her seat, content, until the alarm on her phone went off.

"I need to get that out of the oven, and I have to run it over to Kenni and Baker. They just got married, and I imagine that Kenni is probably overwhelmed with farm life."

She rose from her chair.

Her husband looked up from where his head was bent over the motor. He hadn't said anything since he had told her that he wasn't going on a trip out of the country.

"If you want, I'm almost done here, and I can drive you over."

Smiling, shoving aside any thought of bitterness and only allowing gratitude to show on her face, she said, "I appreciate that."

"Let me get washed up. If you didn't make anything for us, we can go ahead and stop at the diner for supper."

"I do have a small pan set aside for you and me, but I can warm that up tomorrow if you want to go out tonight."

"All right, let's do that."

She nodded, turning and walking into the house. Her husband was a good man. She needed to remember that. But she also had to not allow what he did to affect what she did. She had to do what God wanted her to do, regardless of what he did.

Thank you, Lord, for the reminder. I... I'm sorry to say I needed it. As old as I am, You'd have thought I'd have learned these things by now. Thank you for being patient with me.

Maybe that's all she needed. To be patient with her husband. Maybe, God had good things planned for her, better things than what she could imagine, but He just wanted her submission and obedience in this one little area before He could open the floodgates on the blessings He wanted to shower on her.

The idea made her smile as she grabbed mitts and took the casserole out of the oven.

Chapter 22

Baker pointed his horse toward the farmhouse. Chester was tired, and while his steps were slightly faster because he knew they were headed toward the barn, Baker hated to urge him into a faster gait the way he wanted to, as he was eager to get home to Kenni.

They'd barely gotten the twin fed when a neighbor had called and said his herd of cows had gotten mixed up with his neighbor's, and could he bring his cutting horse over and help get them sorted. He had to go. His neighbor would drop everything to help him if he needed it.

Still, it certainly wasn't the start that he had planned on having for their marriage. It didn't bode well for the rest of it. Although, marriage wasn't a sprint, it was a marathon.

There would be years and years of them being together. But he didn't want to ruin it by starting off badly.

The farmhouse was almost in sight, but Baker's eye was drawn to the pasture.

He didn't groan, but he wanted to.

A cow stood over a little, unmoving black form in front of her. Afterbirth still hanging out.

Obviously she just had it, not even an hour ago.

But the little one in front of her didn't move.

It was very unusual for a newborn calf to not be struggling to get up, almost from the minute it hit the ground.

Baker urged Chester in that direction, his heart sinking.

It was never fun to lose a calf. Also, he had hoped his work for the day was done.

But he couldn't let this one lie in the pasture all night. It would be a magnet for predators, who would possibly become interested in any other calf that looked like easy prey.

Then he remembered the two bottle babies he had at the house. Maybe this mama would take one of those.

She looked up at him, letting out a long, mournful bellow. Almost as though she knew her baby was dead.

In his experience, cows typically didn't know when their babies died, fighting to keep the buzzards and other animals away from calves that have been dead for a day or even two.

Pulling his lariat off the saddle horn, Baker moved Chester toward the nearest gate, leaning down and unlatching it, grateful that Chester had been so well trained by Deuce he was able to open and close the gate without dismounting.

At this point in the day, the less he had to get out of the saddle, the better.

He left the gate unlatched, since he would be dragging the calf out.

The mama cow didn't take too well to him coming over to her calf. She lowered her head, clear that she would be charging him if he tried to get any closer.

He hadn't intended to start his dog like this, but he'd been working with Boomer for a while, and he whined at his feet, ready for the challenge.

Baker said, "Take her back."

Boomer lunged forward and snapped at the cow's head, driving her back, before she chased him with a lowered head.

His dog seemed to know exactly what he wanted and drew the cow away so Baker could come in from behind and wrap his lariat around the hind foot of the little preemie calf.

It didn't take long, and he was back in the saddle in less than thirty seconds.

"Boomer, come on," he said, calling his dog, who left off nipping at the cow and trotted over to his side.

"Good boy," he said, pleased with how he had performed. He'd spent hours training him and was gratified to know that the commands were working, even if he hadn't intended to test his progress out in the field so soon.

He was also thankful he hadn't gotten hurt. That would surely slow down his progress, if they had to work through any fears that might arise from associating cows with pain.

Normally he wouldn't have done what he just did, but he was tired and wanted to get home to his wife. Wanted to make sure that she wasn't upset with him. Wanted to see her smile and know everything was okay between them.

But he couldn't not take care of this cow, and the sooner he did it, the more chance he had of getting one of the bottle babies to take the dead calf's place.

She had plenty of milk and would make a great mom.

He let a lot of rope roll out, so there was at least twenty-five feet between the calf and his horse as they started out of the pasture.

His main concern was the gate, getting out of it, getting the cow out, and then getting back around to get it closed.

Instead of taking his horse back around to shut the gate, he ground tied him and went back to shut it himself.

Just in time, he realized he was a little too close to the calf, and the mama had her head down, coming at him.

It wasn't the first time that had happened, and he was able to scale the fence, hopping over it quickly.

Closing the gate and locking it from the other side, he went a little further up the fence before he hopped back over and got to his horse.

Nothing like a little adrenaline to drive away his feeling of exhaustion.

It had been a long day, and it wasn't nearly over.

Chapter 23

K enni stood on the porch, watching the stars come out.

It would soon be time to feed the bottle babies and get things settled for the night.

She assumed that's what they did. She had no idea of how to go about that.

Last night, they fed the bottle babies, and that had been it. But they hadn't had three baby goats in the barn, along with a brand-new calf, and a steer and a piglet. She still had no idea what to do with them.

The piglet as far as she knew hadn't eaten all day, and it was making oinking sounds, running around the hooves of the steer.

Tempted to text Baker and find out what he was doing, when he was going to be back, and what she should do with everything here, she resisted.

If he wanted her to know something, he knew her number, and she didn't want to distract him when he needed to focus on what he was doing.

She had no sooner thought that than movement caught her eye, up on the high road behind the barn. Baker, on his horse. There was a cow following them. Odd.

Once he got to the other side of the barn, she realized that he was dragging what looked like a...calf. Why would he be dragging a calf?

Her hand went to her heart, then as she watched for a bit more, she realized it must be dead.

"Can you open the gate by the barn?" Baker called out to her, pointing at the gate he meant.

She appreciated the fact that he pointed it out, since there were about seventeen gates around the barn area, and she had no idea which one he wanted.

She ran to the gate, throwing it wide open, and when he called, "Stand back!", she obeyed.

His dog trotted by the horse's heels, the baby calf dragging along behind, the mama cow sniffing, making little mooing sounds, and occasionally bawling. But following along.

She assumed it must be easier for him to bring the cow in by dragging the calf. But she wasn't sure exactly what in the world he would need the cow for. She looked just fine. Of course, Kenni didn't have any idea what signs or symptoms a sick cow would show.

Regardless, he got the calf in the enclosure, and the cow went in right after.

She started to shut the gate, but Baker said, "Hang on a second. I'm going to try to get Chester out, then see if I can't drag this calf out and just leave it right outside the gate."

She did what he said, holding the gate until he got his horse through, then he dismounted, coming back and pulling on the rope until the calf came through.

She thought the mama was going to charge the gate, and her heart felt like it jumped into her throat as she watched to make sure that Baker didn't get hurt.

He latched the gate, letting the calf lie right outside, so the mama wasn't completely separated from it.

"How did it die?" she asked, coming over but still standing well back away from the mama who looked like she could charge the gate at any time.

"I'm not sure. It looks like it might have come a little early, since it's pretty small. But... I don't know."

"Why did you bring it in? Is there a problem with the mom?" she asked.

He shook his head and came over, standing in front of her, his horse's reins in one hand, his other hand going to her shoulder. "Thanks. I...need to apologize again. This wasn't the way I expected our day to go."

"It's okay," she said, appreciating the fact that he took the time to apologize but knowing that if she was going to be on the farm, it was probably best that she had figured out early that things were usually not going to go the way they expected.

"To answer your question, I'm going to skin this calf and put his skin over top of one of our bottle calves."

"Why in the world would you do that?" she asked, taking a step back and barely noticing when his hand fell off her shoulder.

He smiled a little, but his eyes were serious. "It will grow better if it's getting milk from its mom. It just does. We try to make a good substitute for mom's milk, but nothing does better than what God intended. So, he'll gain weight, grow faster, grow better, and get less sick if he's got a mom." He blew out a breath, looking at the dead calf. "Plus, milk replacer is expensive, and it's not going to cost us any more to have this mom in the field with a calf on her than without, but it will save us a good bit in milk replacer."

"I see. So you're going to get the bottle calf to be her calf?"

"Yeah. That's the idea."

"What about the twin?"

It was so sweet and tiny, it could really use a mom.

"I'm afraid it's not sucking well enough. And I don't want to get a mom attached to it and have it not make it."

"I see. You'd have to do it all over again."

"Yeah. I've actually done that once or twice, back on the farm in Virginia growing up, and it's work. But you want to save yourself some time and effort and get the pairing working so you can turn them back out to pasture."

"I see."

"I...wasn't sure whether you'd want to watch this or not."

She bit her lip. He said "skin the calf." She supposed that meant taking a knife and taking the hide off that sweet little baby.

"I guess if I'm going to be a rancher's wife, I need to be able to do the hard things along with the fun things."

"Spoken like a princess."

She laughed. "That's me. The princess."

"Seriously. That's a really great way to look at it. That's pretty much the way life happens, isn't it?"

"It sure is."

"If you don't mind, Chester's had a hard day, and I'm going to take his saddle off, brush him a little, and set him out for the night so he can get a bite to eat before I go to work on the calf."

"You look exhausted," she said, feeling bad for him but not knowing what to do for him.

"It's been a day, that's for sure," he said, not disagreeing.

"Tell me how I can help?"

"Grab a couple pats of hay from the bale that's open on the barn floor, and bring them out to that corral right there where I'm going to put Chester for the night."

"You got it," she said, heading toward the barn where she'd seen the bale of hay open earlier.

She wasn't sure exactly what a pat was, but the answer seemed to be self explanatory when she saw how the bale fell open in slices. She assumed a slice was a pat.

Grabbing three, she noted that the twin was on its feet and bawled a little as she walked by. She assumed that was a good sign but also assumed it was hungry.

"Thanks," he said as she made it to the corral fence, holding the pats of hay. "If you want to just throw them over the fence, that'll be good enough. The trough has water in it, and Chester has everything he needs for the evening."

"That was easy."

"Sure. Although, making those small bales was a ton of work last summer."

She nodded, understanding that there would be work they'd do that wouldn't pay off until months down the road.

"I need to go get my hunting knife. It's in the mudroom beside the kitchen. I'll be right back."

"All right. Mind if I walk with you?"

"I didn't want to ask. I thought maybe you were tired or you'd be offended if I asked you to trot alongside me while I worked."

"Actually, I like it. I suppose, if I had my own work to do, it would be a different story."

"It's always more fun to do work together."

She nodded, thinking that to be true. Every once in a while, she liked to be alone. When she had paparazzi trailing her every move, she appreciated time to be completely by herself. But she agreed with what he said, that working together made things nicer. Sometimes when she had a good helper, it didn't feel like work at all.

Maybe that was what marriage was. Especially on the farm. When there were two people working together, the shared work between them made things lighter and easier.

She liked that idea.

When she had been married to Isaac, she felt like she was working for the crown, and she didn't mind it, but she didn't feel like she and Isaac were a team. It felt very much like she was covering for him, or working to make him look good, but that their goals were not necessarily the same.

She wasn't sure exactly how to explain it, but the idea that she and Baker were together, and together that made things easier, was an easy concept for her to understand.

He grabbed a knife and walked back out of the house, pulling it out of the sheath and running his thumb down over the blade.

"Do you do that to see if it's sharp?" she asked.

"Yeah. You can kinda tell if it's going to work, because it feels...just different than a dull blade."

"That's helpful," she said, laughing.

"I know. I'm sorry." He seemed a little preoccupied, and then he said slowly, "Are you sure you're ready for this?"

"Do you think I shouldn't be?" she threw back at him.

"I don't know. Some people aren't very good with blood and guts and all that stuff. For me, the smell bothers me more than anything. It's not that it's a bad smell, it's just...a dead smell. I don't know how else to explain it."

"All right. I think I'm gonna be fine, although I guess if I'm not... I can leave?"

"Yeah. If that's what you have to do. I would rather you do that than force yourself to stay. Sometimes there are just jobs on the farm that you end up never being able to do."

"I can see myself never being able to do this job, but I guess I'd like to be able to do everything that needs to be done. I want to be a valuable contributor to farm life."

"Don't push yourself too hard. Although, I appreciate it." He glanced over at her, a bit of pride in his eyes, and his lips tilted up, and she loved that look. It made her feel good, like he was happy with the decision that he made.

"I don't want you to think that you married someone who's totally unsuitable for the life that you lead."

"I told you. If we need to, we'll do something else besides farming. After all, you're my wife, and you come before all of this, even though it really feels like you haven't today."

"I think that most days, the work we do is going to be the kind of work that needs to get done. It's not like you can put your wife before hungry calves, or before a goat having babies, or even before the neighbor's emergency."

"A lot of people don't understand that."

"Maybe that's why farming isn't for them."

"There's a lot of reasons why farming isn't for some people. There is a lot of hard work involved. Imagine if we were doing everything we did today, only it was twenty degrees below zero. Or if we were doing everything we did today, and it was ninety degrees. The weather can make everything so much harder."

"I guess we were really blessed to have such a beautiful day, with great temperatures. Even if we did get a pretty wild thunderstorm."

"That wasn't wild, not compared to what North Dakota can typically dish out. I mean, she's got some pretty heavy artillery in her arsenal."

They made it back over to the calf. The cow, standing on the other side of the fence, mooed softly.

"She still wants him."

"That's good. We want her to want him. If she didn't, this would never work."

"All right."

He talked a little as he pulled the carcass toward him, starting almost at the knee of the front leg and cutting the hide around, then carefully taking the skin off, but leaving the membrane, which kept the muscles intact.

"If you leave that membrane there, it makes things a lot less messy. This guy's been dead for a bit, but sometimes they bleed when you cut them."

"I see," she said. "Blood would make everything messier."

"It sure would."

He worked in silence for a bit, as he got one side of the hide off, then he said, "It's kind of important to get the tail. Poop has a pretty strong smell, you don't need me to tell you that, and you really want to get that area so the mama cow can smell it. But you want to be careful up there too. You cut too deep, and you're going to have a mess on your hands."

"All right. We don't have a mess on our hands already?" she asked, smiling. And unable to believe she was actually joking.

But as she thought about it, she realized that she was thinking more about taking this hide and saving a life, getting a mom to accept another baby, giving a baby a chance to have a mom who loved him, rather than two bottles a day from a farmer who didn't have time to give him more attention.

He'd have a better chance at surviving life, plus, it would be better for the farm to raise a healthy, heavier steer.

She understood that pretty easily.

Finally, he had the entire top part of the hide off.

Chapter 24

"Now, we're going to get this carcass out of the way, and then we're going to make holes in the hide so we can tie it around the calf we want her to adopt," Baker said.

Kenni helped him drag the calf they'd just taken the skin off over to the side.

Then she walked beside him as they went into the barn and grabbed a piece of baler twine. He split it in half, made holes in the hide, and tied the baler twine to two holes at the front and back on the left side of the hide.

"When we get this coat on the new calf, we'll bring the ties around, secure it to the other side, and then we're gonna put him in the pen with his mama and see what happens."

"Will he know where to go to suck?"

"Bottle babies usually will suck anything, and I think he'll figure it out. Sometimes, when they've been roughed up, like the twin's mom didn't want him, they're scared of big cows, and they won't go over. If that happens with this guy, we'll have to put her in the head chute and teach him how to drink."

Baker looked so tired, and it had already been such a long day, she really hoped they didn't have to do that. She hoped it would be easy, and the mama would take the baby right away, he'd figure out how to eat, and Baker could go in and sit down.

Only to do it all again the next day.

Except everyone kept saying that days weren't usually this hard.

She had to believe that.

As he opened the gate, he said, "Which one do you think we should try?"

One of them was just a little bit smaller than the other, and he had automatically become her favorite. She pointed to him.

"Good choice. I like that one too." He grinned at her, almost as though he knew that she only chose him because he was just a touch smaller. "Can you put your fingers out and let him suck on your fingers while I get his new coat on?"

"He won't bite?"

"They can't. I mean, if you stick your hands in the back of their mouth, maybe they can, but they don't have front teeth on the upper part of their mouth."

"Do they come in later?" she asked, thinking that they chopped grass off with their front teeth together.

"Actually, cows grab the grass with their tongue. Their tongue has really grippy taste bud type things on it, and they yank the grass off with that."

"Amazing. I don't think I knew that."

"Here I thought that was something that everyone learned in kindergarten."

"Oh, thanks. Now I'm just as smart as your average kindergartner."

"Slightly less intelligent, since you didn't know."

"Wonderful. The first day of marriage, and he already thinks I'm stupid."

"Hey. I never said that."

"I know. I was teasing you."

"It has been quite a day."

"It's not over yet, either."

"I know. I keep thinking that the odds of this fellow going in and figuring out what he's supposed to do right away are pretty low."

"Do you think the mom will take him?"

"I've never seen this coat trick not work."

"Oh. That's good."

"Yeah. Sometimes you just don't have a coat because the calf got eaten or died a few days before you found it. Or sometimes it's the mom who didn't want the baby, then you have a hard time convincing her to take anything. That's the kind of cow that usually goes down the road."

"Down the road?"

"We sell those kind of cows. She can't stick around here if she doesn't want to raise a baby."

"I see." She tucked that information away or maybe pushed it aside. She didn't like the idea that some cows had to go. But as much as she loved animals and as cute as the babies were, it was still a business. If they didn't make money at it, they couldn't keep doing it. It was like any other business, there had to be profit, there had to be money to pay the bills, to buy groceries, and to pay the mortgage. If there wasn't, they wouldn't be farmers for long.

"Sorry. It's just a fact of life on the farm." Baker's voice held compassion, almost as though he understood exactly what she was thinking.

"No. I can see that easily. I guess it's kind of the same as the monarchy. We try to do what we can to help out, but everything is based on money. If we can't make a profit or at least bring some positive attention to our country, there's no reason to keep the institution. It's just a bunch of ceremonies."

"Sure. Only here we're talking about animals."

"Versus people for the institution," she said casually.

"I guess you're right. You'd be out of a job. But we're not selling princesses to the slaughterhouse."

"Oh. So that's what down the road means. Slaughterhouse."

He put his finger to his lips and said, "Shh. The girls do not know that."

"Is that what you call your cows? The girls?"

"When they're being good. I have other names for them whenever they're being contrary."

"I see," she said. "Are these names that we can teach our children?"

"Of course," he said, giving her a look that shouted his innocence, and she wasn't sure whether he was being sarcastically innocent, or truly.

"All right. See if you can keep your fingers in his mouth if he'll follow you to the gate. It'll be easier to lead him like that than to try to push him where we want him to go."

"All right," she said, keeping her fingers in the calf's mouth and walking slowly toward the gate.

It wasn't hard. He followed her, trying to keep sucking while he barely seemed to notice that he was even walking.

"That's perfect. You're natural at it. Just go ahead and take him up to the gate where his new mom is. I'll shut this, and I'll be following right behind you. Hopefully I'll be there in time to open the gate." He paused for just a moment. "Be careful. She's protective, and she'll knock you down if she can."

"All right. I think I figured that out. But I appreciate the warning."

"Yeah, that's the kind of cow I like. Honestly," he said as she kept walking, "we don't want a mama who's not protective of her baby. They're out in the pasture by themselves, and protective moms will keep the buzzards away and protect them from any stray dogs that get through the fence or anything else that comes along."

"Yeah. I can see why having a cow who protects her baby is an asset, not really a liability. Although... I think I've heard of people actually really getting hurt by overprotective mama cows."

"Yeah. I know people personally who have been hurt, and even killed in a couple of instances, by cows that have caught them in the wrong way at the wrong time." He caught up to her and put his hands around her shoulders, holding onto her, lightly, not pulling her into him, just having that contact.

She liked that. Liked the way it showed they were together, almost like they had been talking about earlier. Working together, side by side.

"It's just a matter of making sure you're aware, and trying to anticipate what could happen, and not letting yourself get caught in a bad situation."

"You make it sound easy."

"Well, I think most of the time, accidents happen because we get lax. We think we know what a cow is going to do, and we turn our back on her and don't keep an eye on her like we should. Probably that's the most important thing. You always watch. If you're in a corral or a fenced area with a cow, you keep your eye on her. Especially if she's a new mom. You want to have that awareness so that you can react if the situation starts to get out of hand."

"I see. I'll try to keep that in mind."

"Yeah. Although, I really don't want you working too much around the cows, at least not without me. Not that you can't, not that you wouldn't be really great at it, I just... My job is to take care of you. And I wouldn't be doing my job very well if I didn't try to keep you out of situations where you could get hurt."

"I don't want to see you in situations where you can get hurt any more than you want to see me in them."

"That's my job. You know?"

She could tell he didn't want to say anything more. Probably because he was afraid she would get upset. It seemed to be a sensitive subject with a lot of women nowadays, but she appreciated that. Appreciated the fact that he took the job that God had given him seriously, that he was going to protect her, and take care of her, and defend her, making sure that he took the more dangerous position and gave her the jobs that were less likely to get her hurt.

"Thank you," she said, putting the hand that wasn't in the calf's mouth over top of his hand on her shoulder. "I like that. I like that I know you're going to protect me if you can. It gives me confidence that any job that you give me is probably not going to be a job that I have to be afraid of."

"I hope not. Or at least, I hope you can be confident that I'll make sure, to the best of my ability, that nothing happens to you."

"I think that's about the best you can do, and I appreciate it."

They reached the gate, and he said, "Boomer," to his dog.

Kenni had almost forgotten about the dog who had laid down when Baker had told him to and hadn't moved from that spot.

"He's really well-trained."

"I spent a lot of time working with him. But yeah, he's worth three men on horseback in the field. Or maybe more." He nodded at the cow. "Take her away."

It seemed to take Boomer a minute or two to figure out what Baker was asking him to do, but then he squeezed between the rails of the fence and nipped at the cow's nose, moving her backward far enough away from the gate that Baker was able to open it.

As he unhooked the chain, he said, "When I get this gate open, I'm going to grab the calf and toss him in, then I'm going to shut the gate as fast as I can. Okay?"

"Got it."

She appreciated that he was telling her what he was going to do so she could be watching for it.

She had the calf ready, in position behind him, when the gate opened, so he could grab it and shove it in right away.

The cow let out a bellow and skirted around Boomer.

At the same time, Baker shouted, "That's enough," which seemed to be the command to stop. Immediately the dog backed off and came running over to Baker.

"Good boy," he said, scratching the head as the dog slipped through the rails.

In that much time, Baker had the gate closed and chained.

It happened so quickly, Kenni hadn't really been noticing that he was working on shutting the gate while he was calling the dog off.

"Wow. That really worked well."

"I like it when it works that way. Sometimes, it doesn't." He glanced over, giving her a look that said things could get pretty bad.

She didn't even ask. She followed his gaze back out to the cow, who was sniffing, then licking at her "new" baby.

"Easy peasy, we got the mom to take it," he murmured. "Now, if Junior would just sniff around and find his lunch, we'll be going in to find ours pretty soon."

"About that," she said, not really wanting to admit that supper hadn't worked out quite the way she thought it was going to.

"Sorry. Didn't mean to imply that I was expecting you to cook supper."

"Oh, I was thinking that I would. That it was my job. I'm willing. Just... I wasn't used to getting stuff out of the freezer and cooking it on the same day. And it...isn't ready."

"Not a big deal. We'll figure something out. We can always have eggs and toast."

"Okay," she said, feeling bad, because he had a big day. Of course, she had too. But his just seemed to be harder, and she wished that she had something to feed him so that he could relax once he got into the house and not expect to do more work.

"I don't know. I'm afraid he's not going to get it."

"He does seem to be kind of afraid of her." And indeed, the calf didn't have any interest in the mom at all. Every time she licked him, he walked away from her.

"I didn't want to have to do it, but I think we might have to run her into the chute."

"I'm not sure what that means, but I'm down for it."

"I'm glad. I'll probably need you to give me a hand in order for me to get it done."

"Gladly. I like it when you need me. It makes me feel useful."

"For now. But after a while, you might start to take off when you think I'm looking around needing an extra hand to give me some help."

"I hope not. Isn't that what farming is? We help each other out?"

"It seems like I'm the one who needs a lot more help."

"Yeah. Although, if you end up cooking us supper, that's you helping me."

"True. Glad you look at it like that."

Chapter 25

Baker and Kenni stood by the gate, watching for a few more minutes while the calf kept walking away from the mom.

"All right. How about we feed the twin, feed the other bottle calf, take a look at the goats, and then—"

"We have a piglet, too. I'm not sure if you remember about it?"

"Forgot. Thanks. We'll see what we can do with a piglet, and I guess we need to get Billy some hay. Then maybe I can call Gideon and see what's up with the piglets. It's kinda odd that just one showed up. Hopefully the rest of them are okay."

"I never even thought about that."

"You didn't need to. It's not really our job to take care of it, but since it's here on the farm, we'll take care of it until they come get it."

"It sounded hungry the last time I heard it. If pigs make little oinking noises when they're hungry."

"I bet it is. It probably hasn't had anything to eat all day."

"No. I wasn't sure...what to feed it. I just think of pigs as eating garbage, but surely that's really not true?"

"Well, they will. They'll eat pretty much anything. I don't like to feed them meat scraps, but they'll eat those too."

"Interesting."

"Yeah. I like to try to make them be vegetarians, although we give them milk and cracked eggs."

"You raise pigs?"

"We always had a few on the farm in Virginia growing up."

"Oh. I forgot about that."

"Yeah. I was in the Air Force for six years or so and didn't do any farming then, but I guess you grow up on a farm, and it's kind of in your blood. You might leave the farm, but the farm never really leaves you."

"All those things you learned. You probably never forget them."

"It's like riding a bike." He grinned.

"I guess I'll probably never forget all the things I learned in Corinth, but I can hardly think that those are the kinds of things that are going to help me out in life at all."

"Oh, you never know. You'll probably be able to decorate the farmhouse really well. And if you need to coordinate my outfits, I bet you've got that down."

"I can get you a really nice suit, if you have $10,000."

"Oh, goodness. I sure hope I don't ever have to go anywhere where I need to wear a suit that cost that much. I'd be kind of afraid to do anything besides stand in a corner and keep people from touching me."

She laughed, thinking about how she'd worn gowns that cost even more. Of course, as the People's Princess, she tried to keep her wardrobe accessible and inexpensive.

She had to assume, though, that inexpensive was relative. Since, to her, having an outfit that was less than five hundred dollars and bought off the rack, or rented, was very inexpensive.

She had an idea that even a five-hundred-dollar dress would be expensive for the farm.

But where would she need to go where she would wear clothes like that?

"You think you're going to miss it?" he asked as they turned together, walking toward the house to get bottles.

"No," she said immediately.

"You said that fast. That either means that you really mean it, or you really don't mean it."

"I really meant it." She kicked at a stone, watching as it bounced in front of them. "I loved what I did, don't get me wrong. But it was one of those things where you love what you do because you're doing it and you don't have a choice, you know?"

"Yeah." He laughed. "Where you just reenlist, and you're thinking to yourself what a crazy idiot you are, and you've got three years stretching out like a lifetime in front of you, and you don't have any choice but to suck it up and get started."

"That was you?"

"Not to steal your thunder, but yeah. I shouldn't have reenlisted. I like the Air Force okay, but like I said, farming was in my blood. But those extra three years gave me a little more money to help buy this place, so there was that."

"I see. That makes sense." She thought about the marriage settlement she'd gotten. It hadn't been huge; she hadn't asked for anything extravagant. But it was several million dollars.

She supposed she should mention that to him at some point.

Except...was it theirs? Did she have to share?

She barely knew him. They'd only been married a day. The subject hadn't come up.

She had been so concerned about the idea of them working together, of them shouldering the burden together, wouldn't having the money together be something that they would have too? Wasn't that going along with what she wanted?

A real marriage, a real partnership, a real relationship.

"I guess I have to say that there were a few times this winter, where it was negative forty degrees, when I was lying in bed, cold before I even got up, wondering what in the world I was doing. Surely there's an easier way to live life, you know?"

"You're saying that there will probably be times on the farm, even if we love it, where we have to just put our heads down and keep going?"

"You got it." They had made it to the mudroom, where he grabbed the bottles, saying, "We'll do one and a quarter."

She nodded, taking the bottles from him and measuring out the appropriate amount of milk replacer.

He added the hot water, shaking them both really well before topping them off with the correct amount.

"I guess I would have thought life at the palace would have been all peaches and roses," he mused, and he didn't seem quite as happy as he had. "It must seem like such a comedown to be here on the farm, skinning dead calves and working...has it been twelve, fourteen hours today?"

She glanced at her watch. "I haven't been keeping track."

"That's pretty much every day. If you get downtime during the day, you might be 'on the job,' but you're pretty much on the go until you hit the pillow at night, sometimes you just have to call it quits and realize that you'll pick up the pieces and start again in the morning."

"Well, it's a different kind of schedule. I didn't work quite as hard, and my handlers were always very careful to make sure that they scheduled breaks for me. But I think I like this kind of work better. Although, negative forty sounds pretty cold."

"I'm telling you, you haven't felt cold, till you've felt North Dakota cold."

"I guess I'll find out this winter."

"I guess you will," he said, his eyes sparkling, like he appreciated that she said that, and he hadn't been sure she would stick around long enough.

"I'm not going anywhere," she said, letting her stubborn nature shine through her words.

"I hope not. It's only been a day, and already I hate the idea of not being able to do this with you. I just...hate that we didn't work together more today."

"You don't have to keep saying that. I promise, I'm a big girl, and I can entertain myself if you're busy."

"Seems like you did a pretty good job of entertaining yourself, what with all the kids, Billy, all the people and the goat, and everything else that went on today."

"In fact, maybe I'm a little too good at entertaining myself, come to think of it," she said, as though he'd made her rethink her initial assessment.

He barked out a laugh. "It won't take any time at all to feed this guy. He's an old hand at sucking, and he'll drink it right down." He held out the bottle. "Would you like to do the honors?"

"I'd love to. Does this get old?"

"Not for me it doesn't. I guess sometimes when you've got a stubborn one, that just won't learn to suck, you get a little frustrated, because it does take longer, you tend to get messy, too, but no. Babies don't get old, mama cows taking a newborn calf, none of that gets old. It's a blessing every day."

She could hear the love in his voice. Could tell that this was what he wanted to be doing. This was what he was made for.

She told herself, no matter how cold it got this winter, she wouldn't talk about quitting. Obviously, Baker had been born to be on the farm. For her to ask him to do anything else was for her to ask him to give up a part of himself.

Maybe she hadn't exactly realized that when they got married, but she did believe that it was her job to be beside him, wherever he was meant to be. Maybe the Lord made it so that women more easily adapted to things than men. Or maybe the Lord made it so that while the men had the hard job of protecting and providing, the woman had just as hard of a job adapting and supporting.

Regardless, God knew best, and she certainly wasn't going to argue with her Creator about what He wanted her to do.

"Sometimes you get a little overwhelmed, just because of all the things that happen. Sometimes there's a lot of things to worry about, bills, breakdowns, even droughts and subfreezing temperatures, but... But if you just keep your mind on all that's beautiful, it isn't hard to remember it's a blessed life."

"You might need to remind me of that. I think that's probably true for anything, though, right? I mean, in the palace, I can think about the drudgery of every day. Of having to get up and go out and smile even when I didn't feel like it. Of having my days completely scheduled and not having the freedom to be me, to go where I want, when I want. Or I could think about the good I was doing for people. Focus on the different ways that I could help and be a blessing. To use my creativity within the bounds that I was provided. To be content where I was, and to see the beauty and history that I was so blessed to be a part of. It's just a matter of choice."

"I couldn't have said that better. We don't focus on the heat, the insects, the cold, and the death. We focus on the life." He nodded at the baby in the corral, who still wasn't nuzzling his mother. "Not the death. The life."

As though he was talking about how they didn't focus on the death, on the skin, on the smell, on what they had to do in order to give that cow a baby she could love. They focused on the life. On the blessing of having a mama cow want the baby so bad she would follow it around the pen, making that low, loving mooing sound, just begging the baby to want her.

She thought about how the mom had charged at them, how she lowered her head and wanted to protect her baby. Now that mama was getting a second chance to raise a little one, and that was what she wanted to focus on. Not the calf they had lost, not the life that had to be sacrificed.

"He finished. You're right. That didn't take long at all."

"It will probably take ten times as long for our new little guy, if he won't eat it by himself."

"Maybe he'll suck."

"Maybe. That would be nice." Exhaustion seeped into his voice.

"Then we'll wonder whether we should have put that one on the cow instead of the other one."

"Good point. She would have done a better job of raising him. And since he was a twin, he could use the extra help."

"Too late to change," she said. "That mama has fallen in love."

"We need the baby to fall in love now."

"He will. How can he resist?"

"I think I could," he said, giving her a grin she loved. It made him look boyish and young and wiped a lot of the tired lines from his face.

"You need to smile like that more often," she said.

"I guess if it makes your eyes light up like they are right now, I'll smile however you want me to."

She chuckled, and then she said, "That's funny. I guess that has to do with working together. That...your smile makes me happy, and mine, apparently, makes you happy. That...our attitudes affect each other. That shouldn't be so earthshaking, but it just made me think that on the days where I'm feeling like I want to quit, I don't want that to be infectious."

"Good point. I hadn't really thought about it like that. I mean, we know it. I know that how I act affects the people around me, but I don't usually think about it. That makes sense?"

"Yeah. That's exactly what I'm saying. I just act the way I feel, and I don't stop to think that maybe I'm bringing people down by not shoving those not-so-nice feelings aside and putting a smile on. It lifts people up."

"It sure does. I know you made my heart skip a couple beats when you grinned at me."

"Oh, my goodness. You're such a charmer," she said, rolling her eyes as he held the barn door open and waited for her to walk through.

"I'm serious."

"You're just feeling bad for me because the first day of my new life was a little bit hard. I keep telling you I can handle it, and you keep acting like you don't believe me, but that you have to be all charming and solicitous or I'll... I don't know, I'll cry or something."

"Don't be too hard on yourself. There are definitely days I want to cry. I'm sure you're going to have those days too."

"Maybe I have those moments."

"That's probably a better way to say it. Do you want to give him the bottle?"

"I think you'd better do it one more time. It's a little bit different when they're not sucking."

"You want to make sure they don't breathe it in. You want to make sure they're swallowing. If they're not swallowing, you're not really doing any good by pouring it into their lungs."

"That would give them, what, pneumonia or something?"

"Yeah. Of course, when a calf doesn't really want to live, it's kind of hard to make it. We can tube it, which is when you shove a tube down its throat, careful to get it into its esophagus and not into its larynx, and pour the milk in that way. But typically if you have to tube a calf, they're pretty far gone."

Chapter 26

"Lark sometimes comes out, if we've got a high-dollar calf," Baker said as he held the bottle up.

"The vet?" Kenni surmised.

"Yeah. She's good at what she does."

"Doesn't she also run a home for girls?"

"I don't know that she runs it, so much as people just drop girls off at her doorstep. I've never really heard. But yeah. She always has a bunch of people who aren't related to her hanging around her place."

"Sounds like she's found her place in the world."

"I heard there's some heartbreak in her history. Some...lost love. Or..." He scrunched his nose up, as though trying to figure out exactly what he had heard. "She had a crush on a farmer who was too old for her. I think that's the way it went. Apparently the guy still lives around here, but I've never checked into it."

He lifted his shoulder, like it didn't really matter to him, that he liked Lark, but he wasn't interested in her. Then he went back to focusing on getting his fingers in the calf's mouth, putting the nipple between its upper jaw and lower jaw.

"I try to give him a little taste of milk. Hopefully, he'll decide that he likes it and start to suck. That sucking instinct is one of the strongest. After all, it's the key to survival."

"And if he doesn't suck?"

"We'll do what we did before. I've never had a calf that didn't eventually start to suck. Although, I've had a couple that died. They just…don't seem to have the will to live. Then, you have others that are so far gone you think they'd never make it, and yet they struggle on. Just have that drive. You can't really do it yourself. It's something that's in them."

"Isn't that the way people are?" she asked as he successfully put the bottle in the calf's mouth and started to dump it down its throat.

He didn't answer for a few minutes, almost as though he were thinking. "Like some people just have a zest for life? And some people don't?"

"Yeah. I guess. Or… Some people just go after what they want with both hands. Some people are a lot more content to just relax and take life as it comes."

"What kind of person are you?" Then he lifted his head, without looking back at her, and said, "Wait. Let me guess."

"All right. Guess." She was almost certain he would get it wrong. There was a public persona that she needed to have when she was at the palace. Even when she was a teenager, back when they knew each other, she had a persona that she donned, knowing that her natural personality didn't shine brightly enough to get any attention.

"You're the kind of person who enjoys stepping back and watching. You're a lot more relaxed, laid-back, although you're not afraid to fight for things if you believe in the cause." One side of his mouth pulled back as he looked over his shoulder. "How'd I do?"

"You know what. I couldn't have said it any better."

He laughed. "That's a compliment."

"It surprises me. I didn't think you'd know. Although, I know what you are."

"Yeah?"

"You're in the middle. You're not exactly laid-back, but you're not a fighter either. You'd rather give in and get along, but there are a lot of things you feel passionately about. Including farming."

He laughed. "That's been pretty obvious, so I don't think you get any brownie points for that."

"No? I thought I was pretty observant."

"All right. You're pretty observant. And you get lots of brownie points."

After a few more moments, he pulled the bottle out. "That's it for now. Tomorrow morning, we'll do a quarter of a bottle again. And we'll feed him every four hours, from six in the morning until six at night. I might even come out here around ten and give him another bottle. A quarter isn't too much."

"Someone told me today that if you give a calf too much to eat, you'll kill it."

"Wise person."

They laughed together.

"Where's that extra milk I made?" He looked around, finding it where he set it on the hay bale beside the calf.

"For the piglet?" she asked, and he nodded.

They slipped out the barn door, with Kenni taking one last look at the calf, saying a little prayer that he would make it. He was so sweet, so tiny. So innocent. She wanted to see him have a chance.

But they were doing the best they could. A lot of it was up to him.

As they turned to go toward where Billy had bedded down with the pig beside him, Baker's hand slid into hers.

It made her smile, and her fingers squeezed his, letting him know that she felt it and she liked it.

"I just don't think I could be any happier," Baker said, not talking exactly about their hands but about them in particular. She knew exactly what he was saying.

"It's hard for me to believe. I came here to get away from the paparazzi and the threat of abduction, and... I found a life I'd never dreamed of."

"And I think I'm falling for my best friend's little sister. That violates some kind of guy code or something, doesn't it?"

"Falling?"

"Is that too hard to believe?"

"Maybe. I... I guess I just don't see anything worth admiring in me."

"Maybe you should see yourself through my eyes."

She didn't say anything, and he didn't press the issue as they walked up to Billy, who was bedded down, his head leaning against his side, his one horn stretched over his back.

"Hey there, buddy," Baker said as he squatted down beside him. "Be careful, if he moves his head around, you don't want to be where those horns will hit you. He has never used them to hurt anyone, not that I know of, but I'm sure he'd accidentally knock you over with them."

"Thanks for the warning," she said, scrunching down beside him, slightly behind, to be well out of the way of the horns.

It didn't take much for the piglet to wake up and start snorting, nosing around the ground and eventually nosing onto Baker's hand, looking for something to eat.

"We brought you a little bit of milk, buddy," he said, pouring the bit they brought into the small container he'd shoved in his pocket.

It didn't have to sniff too long before it started to drink, making the cutest little snorting noises while it did.

"I don't know if I've ever seen anything cuter than a baby pig."

"I'd like to have pigs. But they're really hard to keep in. Seemed like our pigs were out more than they were in. In fact, I think we'd have much better luck fencing them out of the pen than in."

She laughed.

"Chasing pigs is not fun. Plus, they bite. They smell. And sometimes it seems like they have more diseases than all other farm animals put together. I know we fought with infant mortality a lot. Seemed like we'd just get something figured out so that our sow would have a good, healthy litter, and then something else would crop up, and you'd lose an entire farrowing pen of baby pigs. It can be heartbreaking."

"And hard on the pocketbook."

"Exactly. You want to have side businesses that don't have a lot of risk but help line your pockets. Maybe making up a little for the year that there's a drought, or where it's too wet to make hay for a month, or where you lose a bunch of cows in a blizzard or something."

"You lose cows in blizzards?" She hadn't considered that.

"Sometimes. Sometimes it just gets so cold their breath freezes over their noses, and they suffocate. A lot of times when it's cold and snowing, you don't have any choice but to go out and check your herd."

"I've heard of people getting lost in the snow."

"That's a danger. Although, we have fences now. Normally you run into one, and you could just follow it until you get to some-place where it looks familiar to you."

"I hope I don't ever have to remember that, but I will anyway."

"Yeah. I don't think there would ever be a time where I would be so desperate to keep things going that I would send you out to check on the herd in a blizzard where there was potential for you to get lost and die."

"I guess you just never know," she said, knowing that sometimes things just didn't work out the way a person planned. Take that day for instance. She certainly hadn't planned on the things that happened, but they made it through.

"I guess that's where faith comes in," she said softly.

He stood hunched over, like he was thinking about it, and then finally he nodded his head. "That's true. Because ultimately, we're not in control of anything. We like to think we are, but it's God who holds the reins on everything."

She straightened, and he did as well. The pig was cute, but her eyes were drawn to her husband.

"Even us," he finally said.

"I was thinking the exact same thing. Our wedding seems like a crazy thing out of the blue, but God knew."

"He did. Kind of hard to believe, but it didn't surprise Him in any way. In fact, you can almost see how He worked things out, with us knowing each other when we were younger. I don't know about you, but that made it easier for me to make a decision. I felt like I knew you, I knew your brother, I...knew your values and morals and the way you were raised."

"Same. Only, you're better now than you were then." She grinned. But it wasn't a carefree grin, it was tempered with all the things that rolled inside of her, feelings she couldn't express, ideas that didn't have enough form for her to articulate them. And emotions. So many, from gratefulness, to a feeling of security, of being held in God's arms, and placed right where He wanted her to be.

Whether the paparazzi found her or not, that wasn't really the point. It shouldn't have been the point all along, but sometimes she got caught up in the flow of her life and forgot that her ship was being captained by God.

"All right. Let's walk back out and see if that baby is trying to get his lunch. Then I think we have everything taken care of," he said, his words seeming a little distracted, and she read in his eyes some of the same feelings she was feeling.

They turned, their hands finding each other and linking between them. It made her smile. Maybe someday they'd walk hand in hand, and it would be as natural as breathing.

Maybe she'd take it for granted, holding his hand. Feeling the strength and warmth beside her. Knowing that she had a partner for life.

They checked in the pen and she could feel his relief when they saw the calf sucking from his new mom who stood, contentedly chewing her cud and looking for all the world like she was as happy as could be.

They shared happy, although tired, smiles as they turned back toward the house.

She almost groaned when headlights came down the driveway.

It wasn't pitch dark, but dusk had definitely settled, as well as a chill that made her shiver.

"Cold?"

"A little."

"It often does get cold when the sky is clear and the sun goes down."

"I'll have to remember that."

"A lot of times, it feels good after the heat of the day."

"I can imagine."

"I thought maybe you were shivering because one more visitor. It seems like this day never ends."

"It wasn't because of that, but it could have been."

"That kind of looks like Miss Helen's car. I think I heard from someone that she was going to make us a meal. I didn't know it was today, or I would have told you."

"Well, if it is, it's perfect timing. Since I was attempting a meal but hadn't gotten very far."

"That's just fine. I think you've done enough for today."

"Have I ever mentioned how much I love having neighbors who drop by unexpectedly, bringing food?"

He laughed. "I have to admit those are my favorite kind of neighbors too."

"I hope that's the kind of neighbor that I am. Eventually."

"I would imagine you'll be better." They took another step, and then he said, "Maybe when you have six kids, it might be better to have someone watch the kids rather than bring food."

"There you are, being charming again."

"I guess it's just my natural personality."

She laughed, but she sobered immediately. "I think it probably is."

"I'm not sure that's a compliment."

"I just don't want you to be charming to the rest of the world. Or maybe too charming. I... I want to be special."

There. Maybe that was one of the things that she felt about Isaac but could never articulate to him. She just felt like she was one of many. That he never treated her like she was any different than any other member of the royal family. It was almost like it was a surprise when she showed up in his bedroom at night.

Back when they shared rooms.

Which, speaking of, as she was thinking about it, she realized that she really wanted to talk to Baker about their sleeping arrangements.

Not that she necessarily wanted to move their relationship forward, she wasn't ready for that, but... It just felt wrong having his friends know exactly what their relationship status was, since they shared a house and they couldn't help but see where she slept at night.

"I think her husband is driving her." Baker sounded surprised.

"Don't they usually go out together?"

"I don't know. Sometimes it seems like they barely talk to each other. I heard rumors... Small town, you know."

"I'm sure people will hear the same rumors about us."

"I'm sure they will. On the one hand, it feels like gossip, but on the other hand, sometimes those rumors can prompt people to help where they might not have known that there was a need before. After all, the fact that you and I got married, and that you might not be entirely comfortable, seems to have provided us with food for tonight."

"That is an excellent point."

She liked the way he saw sides of things that she might not. That he enriched her thinking and made her better. That he had opened up a new world to her. One that, while she knew it was going to be a lot of work, it still seemed fresh and exciting and challenging. She loved the challenge. She couldn't wait to dig in beside Baker and see what life was going to bring them. Or, maybe more to the point, to see what they could make of life.

It was no doubt it was going to be an exciting adventure.

Chapter 27

Baker stood in the bathroom, a towel wrapped around his waist, berating himself.

He never bothered to bring clothes to the bathroom. Half the time, he hung his towel on a hook and just walked to his room without thinking about it.

But he could hardly do that with Kenni here.

It was going to take a little bit of getting used to. He didn't want to embarrass her.

He also didn't want her to think that he was trying to push her into something she wasn't ready for.

Of course, he really wouldn't mind not having the embarrassment of having his wife walk to a separate bedroom every night while his buddies looked on.

That was one aspect of sharing a house that he hadn't considered. Otherwise, he was content to be as patient as she wanted, it was just... He preferred that side of their relationship stay private. Impossible in a house like theirs.

Plus, he could have told her in the morning when he was getting up and talked to her for a bit if she wanted.

Maybe she wasn't a morning person.

He tried not to think along those lines. She'd made the decision, and he'd agreed to go along with it. He needed to honor his commitment.

Wishing he'd at least brought a shirt, he opened the bathroom door and stepped out of the hall.

Kenni was just stepping up the top step, and she froze when she saw him.

The bathroom light was on behind him, so most of his body was in shadow, and it wasn't like she hadn't seen a man without a shirt on before.

She'd been married before, for goodness' sake. It was just...the idea that he didn't want to push her. Hadn't intended to get caught like this.

"Sorry," he said, uncomfortable, hooking a hand around his neck, looking for something to do to keep himself occupied. "I'm not used to having to carry clothes to the bathroom with me, and most of the time, I don't even bother with the towel when I walk to my room."

Man. What in the world was he thinking? Yeah, explaining it like that made it a hundred times better. Not.

"It's okay. I... I was just coming upstairs. I did want to talk to you. I...heard a vehicle, and I think that Miller and Zeke might be coming back."

It was possible. They'd had supper, lingering over their meals at the table, talking and laughing. It felt intimate, even though he knew there would be plenty of meals where they would be sharing their table with his friends.

It wasn't like he was going to snap his fingers and have a house for them. That wasn't even on the table. He'd sunk all of his money into buying the ranch and the cows. He couldn't afford to take what was left in the bank and put it toward anything but the essentials for keeping the farm going until he had feeders to sell.

"They should be back about now. So it probably was them."

"I was coming up because I wanted to say something to you before they got back." She spoke quickly, almost as though she were pushing the words out, like they were hard, or maybe it was just that she wanted to get them out before his friends walked in.

"All right," he said, concerned. She had been so relaxed at supper. So calm and willing to roll with whatever happened. He thought they'd come to a great understanding and that she was content and happy where they were.

But now... Now she sounded nervous and upset again. He wanted to fix it.

He could hear the motor. Apparently she could too, because she moved forward.

He froze, aware that he still stood in a towel.

She must have noticed, because her eyes dropped to his shoulders and ran over his chest before she looked back up at him. "Baker?"

"Hmm?" he said, unable to get his tongue to work as she put her hand on his shoulder.

He didn't flinch, but he almost felt like he wanted to. Not that he didn't want her to touch him, just that it was so unexpected.

"I don't want you to get the wrong idea."

He wasn't sure what idea he was supposed to be getting, but he supposed that the ideas that were floating through his head were probably all the wrong ones.

"All right," he said, when she didn't say anything more. His throat was dry. The word wasn't a squeak, but it didn't sound normal.

"I was thinking that it might be better for us to share a room."

His heart stopped. His breath froze in his lungs, and his hand, which had been hooked around his neck, moved of its own accord across her cheek, with his fingers burying themselves in her hair at the nape of her neck.

"The wrong idea?" He managed to get half a sentence out anyway.

"I... I think it's too soon to..."

"Yeah?" he prompted again. If he wasn't fighting himself so hard to keep from pulling her against him, he might think the whole exchange was funny. Her stumbling over her words, and him hanging on every one of them, unable to fathom what in the world she might be going to say and just repeating everything she said like he had no brain of his own. Which, it did kind of feel like his brain had left his body for the moment.

"I thought it was none of your friends' business to know what's going on in our relationship. If I stay in my own room, they're going to know exactly where we stand. If I move into yours, even if we don't..."

"All right. I think I see." His fingers tightened on the back of her head, her hair soft against his skin. You want to share a room but not a bed?"

"Well, I don't really want you sleeping on the floor." She bit her lip, a little smile tilting her mouth. "I don't want to sleep on the floor either."

"All right. We just sleep on separate sides of the bed?"

"Yeah. Kind of."

"Kind of?" He lifted a brow and then shut up as her hand landed on the bare skin of his rib cage.

"Well. I wouldn't mind snuggling."

He grinned, shaking his head. "I don't know if I want to snuggle."

Her face turned down, despite his smile, and he used a finger to tilt her chin up.

"Snuggling is probably not a good idea if we're supposed to be sleeping on different sides of the bed. But eventually, I definitely would like to snuggle."

"Oh."

He was delighted with the twinkle that lit her eyes, but he wasn't sure if she was going to say anything, because his mouth was already lowering toward hers.

He thought maybe he heard the door opening, and he supposed he should forget about kissing his wife and work on getting himself to his bedroom without losing his towel, but his rational brain really wasn't working.

He seemed to have that problem whenever Kenni was around.

"I hope that means it's okay if I kiss you?" he said softly, his lips close enough to hers that they brushed as they moved.

"I was hoping you would," she said, lifting herself up just a little so their lips no longer brushed but touched.

His hand went from her chin to around her waist, pulling her closer and kissing her the way he'd wanted to all day.

The hall disappeared, so did the aches in his body, the tiredness of his muscles, the exhaustion that had pulled at him for the last few hours, replaced by the woman in front of him. The one who had pledged her life to his and then had met every challenge she'd been presented with all day long.

He figured God knew what He was doing when He brought them together. That He found the perfect woman to be a farmer's wife. Even if she had been a princess.

Even if he wouldn't have thought to choose her out of all the women in the world. God knew and had brought him the very best.

"I think you guys are going to need to build your own house," a voice said from the top of the stairs.

"I think that's a good idea," Baker said, knowing his voice sounded husky and breathless but not even trying to hide it.

"Maybe we shouldn't do this in the hall," he said to Kenni, hoping she would go along with him as he took a step, grabbing her hand. He walked to his bedroom, casting one short glance at the look on Miller's face as they passed.

His lifted brows settled into a smirk as he shook his head, turning to go back down the steps. "I guess you're not going to care if I eat the rest of the leftovers."

"I guess you're right," he said as he waited for Kenni to follow him through the door before he closed it on his friend.

"Thank you," he said as he leaned back against the closed door, looking at the woman who had married him without question, then followed him into his bedroom without protest.

"I guess that means yes to my question?" she said, and instead of standing where she was, she came back, putting both hands on his chest.

"Like I would have said anything else," he said with a smile that was probably more wolfish than anything.

"I didn't know for sure."

"Now you do."

"I... I don't want you to get the wrong idea—"

"I'm reminding myself that I need to not get the wrong idea. Trust me." He was most definitely reminding himself that he needed to take things slow with her, that even though she followed him into the bedroom, nothing else had changed.

"But I was hoping we could practice kissing a little more. It was...nice."

"Just nice?" he asked, pretending to be offended.

She lifted a shoulder, giving him a glance, a quick glance. "Well, there were elements of potential."

"There's...potential in my kiss?"

"Yes. There was definitely potential there. I can...see with some practice, you might actually get quite good at it."

"Quite good?"

"Is there a parrot in the room?" she asked, glancing around.

"Kind of feels that way, doesn't it? You might have thought the kiss was just nice, but for me, it turned my brain to mush. I apparently can't come up with my own sentences and have to repeat yours."

"Wow. Now that's a compliment a girl could get used to."

"Hopefully that's a compliment you'll be returning after I get a little bit of practice under my belt."

"The last time I checked, you weren't wearing a belt."

"Good point."

They laughed together.

"I suppose tomorrow, after your friends have left for the day, I can move my things over here."

"Seriously, we can put pillows down the middle of the bed, or I can throw some blankets on the floor. It's not like I've never slept on the floor before."

"Oh. About that."

"Yeah?"

"Well. I was thinking about this earlier today, and with all the excitement of the wedding and everything, I forgot to tell you that I have a couple of million dollars in a Swiss bank account. I thought maybe we should fill out the appropriate paperwork and put your name on that account as well."

He froze.

Part of him wanted to jump up and down with excitement. Part of him automatically wanted to protect her.

"No. You just keep it. If anything ever happens to us—"

"No. I'm not going to operate like that. Not going to keep something back, not giving everything but that. If something ever happens to us, then it will be both of us going down. It's not going to be me having a little nest egg that I hold back just in case something happens. Maybe that's crazy, but that's not the way to go into a relationship. Into a marriage. You're getting everything I have. It's all yours."

He didn't know what to say. He felt...humbled. He didn't have millions of dollars. He didn't even have a hundred thousand dollars. All he had was a farm that he shared with his buddies.

"You're giving too much," he finally said.

"No. It's not. I'm not giving anything more than you. Are you giving everything you have?" she asked, tilting her head.

"I don't have that much."

"So a hundred percent?"

"Everything I have is yours." He held his hands up, indicating they were empty, that that was all he could offer.

"Then I give a hundred percent, too. And we're equal."

"That's not the way you should look at that. You know that."

"Are we really having our first serious argument? Is this a fight? Should I write in my diary tonight we had our first married couple fight?"

"Over money, too. Isn't that what married couples always fight over? Money?"

"Let's be different. Let's not fight."

"You stop disagreeing with me, and then we won't."

"Hold up. When I'm right, you have to agree with me."

"Well, in this case, you're not right."

"But I am. We both give one hundred percent. Sometimes, in a relationship, you have to give more. Just I'm committed to giving whatever it takes."

"I'm committed to that too."

He could have told her he was committed to a lot of other things. Protecting her, taking care of her, keeping her safe, doing everything he could to make her life easier and better, but... He knew that there were just going to be days that were hard. No matter what he did.

Those were the days that scared him.

But she stood before him, brave and serious. She was literally offering him everything and telling him that what he had was enough.

He wasn't sure he had done anything to deserve it, and it reminded him a little bit of the sacrifice of the cross. He hadn't done anything to deserve that either. But God just smiled and blessed him more than what he deserved. He supposed he ought to just say thank you. Then do everything in his power to be the kind of man who deserved the kind of woman that God had given him.

"Thank you."

She smiled, a little smug. "Now. Some more practice?"

"Yeah. Let's practice some more. I want to move well beyond the nice stage."

"You have potential. I'm willing to help."

"All right, Princess. Let's see what you've got."

He lowered his head toward hers, and she smiled at the nickname. He hoped she would be okay if that was what he called her for the next fifty years.

Enjoy this preview of *Just a Cowboy's Fairy Tale,* just for you!

Just a Cowboy's Fairy Tale

Chapter 1

"Look at the camera and smile."

Eliza Walton took her own advice, looking at Melinda Watts, who held her phone up, snapping pictures of her beloved son, Randy, who sat on Billy, the famous matchmaking steer of Sweet Water, North Dakota.

Billy was moonlighting on his second job today. That of petting zoo star.

Somehow, Eliza had gotten nominated to be in charge of Billy for the end-of-summer Harvest Festival.

"You did great, honey," Melinda said as she came over, her arms outstretched to Randy.

"I want to stay on," Randy said, sticking his lower lip out.

"But there's a whole line of children. We have to let everyone have a turn," Melinda said, very reasonably.

Eliza could see that Randy wasn't the slightest bit interested in the logical argument his mother used.

"Everyone who gets a picture with Billy also gets a lollipop. Kenni is handing them out right over there," Eliza said, pointing to her good friend Kennedy, who had recently married Baker Lawrence.

Funny that she and Kenni would end up being such good friends, considering that she was a reporter—ex-reporter—and Kenni had spent the last decade running from the paparazzi.

That was probably part of the reason why Eliza had quit her job. She had never been part of a pack of paparazzi, chasing famous people, trying to get that one pic that would make her rich. But she had made a living writing stories about people who hadn't necessarily wanted stories written about them.

She had been dissatisfied in her job for a long time, but her friendship with Kenni had solidified her decision to leave Houston and move to Sweet Water.

Crazy decision, according to all of her city friends, since she had no job lined up.

Unless one counted what she was currently doing, being the keeper of the petting zoo, but it didn't pay.

She grinned engagingly at Randy, grateful that she and Kenny had discussed the fact that many children wouldn't want to leave the steer and that they would need something to entice them. The lollipops had been a great idea.

Randy looked over at Kenni, who held a lollipop up, her exposed teeth blue. After giving the steer a last hug, Randy hopped down and ran over, demanding a blue lollipop. His hapless mother followed, after shooting an apologetic yet grateful smile at Eliza.

"You're a popular boy," Eliza said, petting Billy's neck.

The steer stood contentedly chewing his cud, seeming oblivious to all the noise going on around him. He was a natural for the petting zoo.

Eliza had heard all the stories about him being a matchmaking steer, but she felt that was just something small-town people had a tendency to exaggerate.

Being from the city, she was a lot more jaded and certainly a lot more skeptical about stories that had no basis in actual fact.

A matchmaking steer? Cute.

"Who's next?" she asked, turning back to the line of children.

A sweet little girl timidly raised her hand.

"I think Billy loves ponytails," she said as she walked to the little girl, looking at her mom before kneeling down. She had already had several children who wanted to ride but were scared, and chatting with them a bit first helped ease their fears.

The girl grinned broadly and touched her hair. "Like mine?"

"Just like that. And you have two, which should make Billy extra happy."

"Mommy did it," the little girl said, tugging on her mother's hand.

"And she did an excellent job," Eliza said, gently touching the shiny curls that looped out of the tight ponytails.

"Does Billy really like ponytails?"

"He seems to. I think he likes little girls better than little boys too." She lifted her eyes and looked down the line at the assortment of boys and girls still waiting. "But don't tell anyone," she said, her voice lowered to a conspiratorial whisper, drawing the little girl in to her by sharing a secret.

The little girl shrugged her shoulders and ducked her head, giggling a little.

"My name's Eliza," Eliza said, holding out her hand.

The little girl looked at it. "I'm Chloe," she said, still not sure what to do with Eliza's hand.

"You're supposed to shake her hand, Chloe," her mother said, her hands on her shoulders as she leaned down over her daughter.

"Oh," Chloe said, carefully reaching out and taking Eliza's hand.

Eliza gave her a squeeze and a little shake before she said, "Are you ready to pet Billy?"

"I want to ride him. But I want to see you do it first."

"Me?" Eliza said, feeling a strange twist in her stomach. So far, she'd gotten quite used to petting Billy. All he did was stand there and chew, occasionally grabbing another bite of hay from the large pile in front of him. But as for actually getting on his back, she hadn't done it, hadn't planned on it, and, if she were being honest, definitely didn't want to.

"She always feels better if she sees someone else do it first. Someone she trusts," the mom said over Chloe's head, her hands still on both shoulders.

It was on the tip of Eliza's tongue to suggest that the mom get on Billy, but she supposed that as the zookeeper, she was probably the one who ought to set the example.

She wasn't exactly an expert at working with children, but she figured that she could hardly expect a child to do something that she wasn't willing to do herself.

It just seemed reasonable that she would be the one who would have to get on Billy's back.

"Billy is actually quite tame," she said as she stood up, smiling with what she hoped was reassurance.

Despite the fact that her own stomach was writhing in anxiety and fear.

She had just barely gotten comfortable standing beside Billy and petting his head. The idea of getting on his back was...quite scary.

She could understand Chloe's hesitation.

But she had also put at least twenty other children onto the steer's back. She'd done it without thinking about whether or not it might be scary and especially hadn't thought about whether or not she wanted to do it herself.

How could she put all of those other children on the steer and expect them to be okay, if she wasn't willing to do the same thing?

Feeling a little guilty because she had expected young children to do something that she wasn't quite sure she was willing to do, she took a step back and made her smile grow even bigger.

"If it will make you feel better, I can show you how to do it." She was surprised at the confidence in her voice. Of course, after working at the newspaper for so long, she'd developed a bit of an ability to bluff.

She was using every ounce of that ability right now.

The little girl nodded her head, an exaggerated up-and-down motion which made her pigtails bounce like happy little blonde bubbles.

She was so sweet, and she tugged at Eliza's heart. Children had been something that Eliza had never thought about. She had been focused on her career, climbing a ladder, being successful, but... She wasn't even sure what her definition of success was anymore. Was it taking pictures of people who didn't want their pictures taken? Selling them to outlets where they would be plastered all over the world, against those people's will?

Of course, some people wanted to be famous. They wanted to be able to make money from their popularity and charm, so taking famous people's pictures hadn't felt like such an invasion of privacy.

But the line had blurred to the point where she didn't feel comfortable doing it anymore. As long as there was money in it, there would always be someone who was willing, but...that person wasn't going to be her. Not anymore.

"Are you going to do it today?" the little girl asked and not in a sarcastic way. Maybe just in a way that said that sometimes it took her a little bit of time to get her nerve up, so maybe it was taking Eliza a little bit of time as well.

"I'm sorry. Of course. You're just so cute, you made me think about kids and how much fun they are."

Of course, she wasn't so naïve as to think that children weren't a lot of work as well.

A *lot*.

Still, she wasn't going to have children without a husband. And a husband hadn't been even a remote possibility. Most of the men she knew were just as disinterested in families and children as she was.

It was kind of the new modern thing to just hook up but have no plans to actually get together in a permanent way, create a family, and nurture new little humans.

The idea was actually kind of scary.

But not quite as scary as getting on the back of the steer.

She looked at the mother of the little girl and held out her hand again. "I'm Eliza, and I'm not sure who you are."

"Jasmine. And I'm sorry. I should have introduced myself and introduced you to Chloe. I'm not used to adults getting down on her level and making her feel so comfortable."

"She's a sweetheart."

"Thank you. She is a little bit shy, and I appreciate you being willing to show her that there's nothing to be afraid of."

"Of course not. Billy's had dozens of kids on his back already today. But if you wouldn't mind holding him, not that I think he's going anywhere, just to let him know he's not supposed to." Hopefully her smile was hiding all of the nerves that were chasing each other around down in her stomach.

"Of course. I'm sorry. I should have offered."

"It's okay. This isn't like something that we're used to doing every day. At least I'm not."

"Me either. I'm just happy that Chloe has the opportunity. If you don't live on a farm, it's kind of hard to find cows to pet."

"I think for people who live on a farm, it's still hard. Sometimes."

Jasmine laughed. "That's probably true."

Billy wasn't that tall, and Eliza was pretty sure she could stand at his side, jump on his back so that her stomach was up over the top, and then swing a leg over.

Not that she'd ever done anything like that before, but that was her strategy anyway.

"Are you ready?" she asked Jasmine, on the pretense of making sure she was situated. But in actuality, Eliza was just giving herself a little bit more time. She wasn't sure, first of all, that she could get the whole way up on Billy's back. And then, she wasn't sure whether she wouldn't just fall off.

Then, there were the horns. They were huge. At least they seemed that way. And she didn't think that Billy would try to use them on her, but if someone tried to jump on her back, and she had horns that looked like that, she couldn't guarantee she wouldn't use them to at least brush the person off.

How could she expect Billy to be any different?

"Ready," Jasmine said with a smile, holding Chloe with one hand while her other hand held the lead rope that was attached to the rope halter around Billy's face.

She'd procrastinated enough. Eliza took one step closer to Billy and put both hands on his furry back.

He didn't move a muscle. His mouth kept going up and down, and he didn't even look around to see what was going on behind him.

She leaned a little of her weight on him, and again, he didn't move.

Taking a deep breath, she braced her arms, bent her legs, and jumped as high as she could, pushing with her hands, to get her stomach up on his back.

She did such a good job she almost did a head dive off the other side, and it took her a couple of seconds to catch her balance on his back.

Through all of that, Billy never twitched, as though he had people jumping on his back all day long every day and he was used to it.

Which was a good thing, because she needed the extra time to catch her balance.

She lay there over Billy's back, feeling like an idiot, with her head further down the other side than she was comfortable with.

Finally, after he didn't move at all, she pushed her torso up some while trying to swing her right leg over.

She felt about as awkward as she had ever felt in her life before and figured that there was probably a crowd of people standing around laughing at her, but as she straightened up, no one seemed to notice other than Jasmine, who stood with Chloe in front of her, still holding onto Billy's rope.

People mingled, laughing and talking, and the beautiful North Dakota fall sun shone down. Everything seemed to be going on as normal, and no one even stopped to notice that Eliza Walton, world reporter and city girl extraordinaire, was currently sitting on the back of a cow.

There should be trumpets playing or something.

She had no sooner thought that than Billy, who hadn't moved a muscle for the last two hours, casually took first one step then another, and then more as he moved away from the hay and pushed through the rope that had sectioned off his part of the petting zoo.

"Um, Eliza?" Jasmine said with just a little panic in her voice. "What should I do?"

"Can you stop him?" Eliza asked, hearing the same note of panic in her own voice. She had no idea what to do. She'd never...led a cow before. Was that what it was called?

"I'm pulling, but he's not stopping." Jasmine now had both hands on the rope, her daughter Chloe standing beside her with her fingers in her mouth. She had a worried look on her face, although Eliza only glanced back for a moment before she swallowed the lump that had clogged up the back of her throat and buried both hands in Billy's hair.

She wasn't sure exactly what to do, but she wasn't going to jump off, not while he was moving at a leisurely walk that felt more like a stampede, and she was hoping she wasn't going to fall off either. That was what the handfuls of hair were for.

"Stop?" It sounded more like a question. Like she was asking Billy if he felt like stopping today.

He gave the equivalent of a no, as he shook his head just a little, his horns waving back and forth, before he continued walking.

"I'm sorry, but I have to let go!" Jasmine said before she did exactly that.

Billy stepped out onto the sidewalk and casually, slowly moseyed up the street, like he normally took his human for a walk at this time of day.

Eliza, who had been in town for more than two months, knew it to be not true. She'd never seen anyone other than children sit on Billy. Why had she thought she should be the first adult to do so?

She felt trapped. She couldn't get off, she couldn't get him to stop, and she didn't know what to do.

Then, to her horror, Billy started to trot.

Trot, gallop, or something. He started to go faster, and her butt started to bounce. It wouldn't have been too bad, if she would have bounced in the same spot. But the problem was, every time she bounced she came down on a completely different spot, then bounced again, landing in a different spot, until she had bounced to the point her butt was sitting more on Billy's ribs than on his backbone, her leg over the side of Billy's back dug in, trying to hold on, while her hands that had gripped his fur pulled even tighter.

It felt like Billy was going like the wind on the sidewalk, but her logical mind told her he was a cow, and he wasn't going that fast.

Eliza didn't know what to do; she didn't want to fall off. And she didn't want to let go, and she was pretty sure that she wanted to stay calm and cool and collected, but she was pretty sure the scream that reached her ears came out of her own mouth.

She also was fairly certain that she was about to die.

Pick up your copy of *Just a Cowboy's Fairy Tale* by Jessie Gussman today!

A Gift from Jessie

View this code through your smart phone camera to be taken to a page where you can download a FREE ebook when you sign up to get updates from Jessie Gussman! Find out why people say, "Jessie's is the only newsletter I open and read" and "You make my day brighter. Love, love, love reading your newsletters. I don't know where you find time to write books. You are so busy living life. A true blessing." and "I know from now on that I can't be drinking my morning coffee while reading your newsletter – I laughed so hard I sprayed it out all over the table!"

Claim your free book from Jessie!

Escape to more faith-filled romance series by Jessie Gussman!

The Complete Sweet Water, North Dakota Reading Order:
Series One: Sweet Water Ranch Western Cowboy Romance (11 book series)
Series Two: Coming Home to North Dakota (12 book series)
Series Three: Flyboys of Sweet Briar Ranch in North Dakota (13 book series)
Series Four: Sweet View Ranch Western Cowboy Romance (10 book series)
Spinoffs and More! Additional Series You'll Love:
Jessie's First Series: Sweet Haven Farm (4 book series)
Small-Town Romance: The Baxter Boys (5 book series)
Bad-Boy Sweet Romance: Richmond Rebels Sweet Romance (3 book series)
Sweet Water Spinoff: Cowboy Crossing (9 book series)
Holiday Romance: Cowboy Mountain Christmas (6 book series)
Small Town Romantic Comedy: Good Grief, Idaho (5 book series)
True Stories from Jessie's Farm: Stories from Jessie Gussman's Newsletter (3 book series)
Reader-Favorite! Sweet Beach Romance: Blueberry Beach (8 book series)
Cowboy Mountain Christmas Spinoff: A Heartland Cowboy Christmas (9 book series)
Blueberry Beach Spinoff: Strawberry Sands (10 book series)